Devil / Deil
By A G Mallagh
April 2014

Text copyright @ 2012 A G Mallaghan
All Rights Reserved

To my family and friends for their support and encouragement. I don't need to mention any names as you know who you are and your support has been appreciated.

Thank you for downloading Devil / Deil. I hope you enjoyed reading this book and would welcome your feedback. If you could leave a review for this book on Amazon it would be greatly appreciated.

If you are interested in receiving information about forthcoming titles then please email your interest and email address to agmallaghan@hotmail.co.uk or leave a comment at agmallaghan.wordpress.com

Once again thank you very much for taking the time to read this book and hopefully you will enjoy my future stories.

Best Wishes

A G Mallaghan April 2014

Table of Contents

Devil / Deil
Prologue
Chapter 1 Nedfest
Chapter 2 A Few Days Earlier
Chapter 3 The University Dig
Chapter 4 The Electric Compound
Chapter 5 The Post Office
Chapter 6 Further Into the Mountains They Go
Chapter 7 Cothqon
Chapter 8 Teresa
Chapter 9 Seige Over
Chapter 10 Rescue Arrives
Chapter 11 The Camp
Chapter 12 A Conversation
Chapter 13 Teresa and the Priest
Chapter 14 More Survivors
Chapter 15 A Plan is Hatched
Chapter 16 a Sudden Attack
Chapter 17 Time to Move Out
Chapter 18 A Short Journey
Chapter 19 Clearing Out Cothqon
Chapter 20 Arrival at the Compound
Chapter 21 The Chapel
Chapter 22 Assessing the Situation
Chapter 23 Training Day
Chapter 24 Clash of Personalities
Chapter 25 An Update
Chapter 26 The Boss is Informed
Chapter 27 More Deaths
Chapter 28 Settling Down for the Night
Chapter 29 Fox in the Chicken Coop
Chapter 30 Charlies Three and Four
Chapter 31 Bob
Chapter 32 Whitehall
Chapter 33 Fox Hunt
Chapter 34 Jamieson

Chapter 35 A Bomber Launches
Chapter 36 Broken Arrow Explained
Chapter 37 Back to Cothqon
Chapter 38 Charlie Two and the End Game
Chapter 39 Debriefing
Epilogue

Prologue

Southern Scotland September 1940

The weakening sun struggled to pierce the shade of the wizened old trees that almost engulfed the ruins of the church as the day grew to a close. Birds took to the air in a flutter of fear as the powerful diesel engine of an army truck revved loudly. A sergeant in khaki combat dress came running from the church entrance carrying a detonator device trailing cable behind it. A couple of his troops reached out from the back of the truck and helped him up into the vehicle. He glanced at a young serious looking officer who nodded his consent and then he depressed the plunger on the detonator.

There was a loud muffled bang from deep underground followed by a series of consecutive smaller explosions each one nearer to the surface than the one before until finally a small bang let out a cloud of dust from the doorway to the church causing the lintel to collapse partially bringing down the wall and sealing the entrance. The officer had one last look towards the church then at his Sergeant. He then made his way to the front of the truck and banged the glass that separated the troop compartment from the driver's cab. At this signal the driver floored the accelerator and the truck sped down the track to take them out of the hills and back towards their camp. The soldiers of the Occult Bureau were glad to see the old village of Deil get further and further behind them. The officer hoped that they had succeeded in burying the evil that lay there for eternity but he wasn't certain they had.

Chapter 1 Nedfest

Ally Maxwell snorted loudly as he swallowed the last drop of *Buckfast*. He had been drinking heavily the last few weeks since he had been informed that he had HIV. He wasn't sure how he could keep it hidden but he knew he would get no sympathy in his local area. His friend Boogie accelerated the Subaru Impreza round the last corner before the Scottish Power compound. Boogie pulled on the handbrake and brought the car to a halt. All four youths staggered from the powerful saloon and brought more alcohol with them. Ally laughed out loud as Boogie shouted at the compound building in that strange nasal voice that all neds seem to learn.

"Hey, ya bunch of faggots want to come out and play?"

One of the other youths finished his can of lager and threw it over the high security fence towards the buildings.

"Fucking great idea man." Shouted Ally and threw his can as well.

The remaining two did the same then Boogie turned back to the car shouting.

"Come on you bunch of queers let's go down and annoy the Indiana Jones nerds at the loch. This is pure pish man!"

He climbed into the car and accelerated away before the last youth could close the car door.

Ally patted the back of Boogie's chair as they pulled up near a neat row of tents on a small rise overlooking the loch.

"Looks like they're sleeping! " He laughed. "Let's give these fucks a fright, man."

His lanky companion had a leering expression. "Maybe some of the girls are hot "

"Aye some uni totty ha ha." Ally grinned.

They all climbed out of the car and walked towards the tents with the arrogant swagger of a heavyweight boxer that only a thin Scottish ned can carry off.

Boogie burped and covered his mouth. The others sniggered.

Ally ran up to a tent and threw himself onto the roof of it so that it collapsed.

"Wakey, wakey!" He howled, and the others held their sides as they laughed. Ally stood up as he realised he wasn't getting a response from the tent.

"What the?" He kicked the tent and saw it was empty.

Boogie stood watching, drinking from a can of *Red Bull* as the other two circled the tents.

"Ally, something's no right man." He ventured.

Ally shrugged and then walked to the second tent. He slowly zipped down the entrance with a silly smile on his face. "Anyone home?"

He opened the zip and stuck his head inside shouting. "Hello!"

Boogie's eyes widened and he dropped his can as Ally's legs left the ground and he seemed to dive into the tent. He walked slowly towards him wondering how he had managed that strange dive. Then, he suddenly halted when he heard two screams from the tents at the end of the tent row. "Guys don't mess about," he called. "The uni folk aren't here - let's head home." He turned back to the tent. Ally's trainer clad feet stuck out from the entrance at a weird angle. He gave one of the feet a light kick.

"Ally come on let's go. We'll leave those two poofs behind. We'll see how brave they are cutting through the forest on foot at night, man."

There was no response from Ally. A small chill began to work its way up Boogie's spine. He tapped the foot once more then realised his old mate might have done something stupid like knocking himself out when he dived in the tent. He grabbed the ankles and pulled. Ally came out slowly bit by bit and at first Boogie thought he had been correct until he got to the head and shoulders.

Even in the poor light given off by his car headlights Boogie quickly saw the blood around Ally's neck. He leant in to check if his friend was okay and that was when two strong pairs of arms grabbed him and drew him into the darkness. Boogie screamed but a vice-like hand covered his mouth.

Chapter 2 A Few Days Earlier

John Strauss removed his spectacles and rubbed the bridge of his nose. Most people thought that the life of a planner for a local authority was a boring existence, simply looking over plans and writing policies about the infrastructure of towns and villages. What they didn't realise was the pressure that a Head of Planning and Building Control could come under from politicians and businessmen, to agree to developments that stretched the rules and sometimes were plain illegal.

On this front, this particular day had been an absolute bitch. He glanced at the clock on the far wall of his Spartan office and was glad to see it was almost half past two, and that the day would not last much longer. Perhaps he would have an easy last few hours and he could get home to peace and quiet or perhaps get some Christmas shopping done. His little reverie was interrupted by raised voices in the secretarial area. John stood up and had made it half way across the room when his door was thrust open and a large man with a shaven head burst through.

"Thank you, Madame that will be all." The man ordered in a curt manner to Laura the secretary who had followed him into the office

She looked pointedly at John who nodded and she left shaking her head slowly. The powerfully built man closed the door behind him and advanced on the short mullet haired head of planning. "What the hell did you think you were doing? Allowing the university to carry out the dig?"

"Excuse me?" John blurted, trying not to shrink back in his chair. "But who are you?"

The man reached inside his suit jacket and for a horrible second John genuinely thought he was going to produce a gun. Instead, he brought out a wallet similar to those John had seen in countless detective movies and handed it to him. Instead of a police id though John saw that this identified the man as Colonel Tim Forbes of something called the Occult Bureau in the army. John politely handed the wallet back and sat down in his seat, he gestured for Forbes to sit in the seat opposite but Forbes declined the offer.

"Can we at least discuss this like civilised adults Colonel? I assume they still behave like human beings in the army?"

Forbes leant forward onto the desk his knuckles resting on the piles of paper there. He stared intently into John's eyes. "Mr Strauss I do not have the time for idle chit chat. I have responsibility for the security of the former village of Deil next to the Black Loch. I have now learnt that you," He pointed a finger at John for emphasis, "You have decided to give the okay for a University archaeology team to carry out a dig there. Now what part of *prohibited area* did you not understand my friend?"

Forbes cocked his head to the side in the manner of a dog trying to understand its master. John did not know what to say, he did not know of anyone allowing a university team into the Black Loch area the rural team leader must have sanctioned it. He weighed up his options and decided to be honest.

"Colonel, I did not know about this. I didn't sign off for anyone to enter the area and I can only imagine one of my area managers did this."

"What about Scottish Power being allowed in the area then my friend? That particular authorisation has the signature of John Strauss on it."

John swallowed noticeably, his throat felt like sandpaper.

"I did sign that one but they were setting up a compound on the forestry road and were carrying out work on the hills for a wind farm. They were not within the exclusion zone and their routes did not take them through the exclusion zone so I signed it off. I took personal charge of it to be sure of things. I can't believe that my team leader in the area did not inform me of the dig." He shrugged.

"But he's new to here and probably did not realise the importance of reporting to me on any requests for works within the exclusion zone. What can I say Colonel? I am sorry."

"You are sorry," Forbes snarled, "You are fucking sorry?" Some spittle from him struck Strauss' cheeks as Forbes leant further forward until his face filled all of Strauss' vision.

"The University have lost contact with their team and Scottish Power has reported that their men did not call in at the post office today. I would suggest that you consider your position Mr Strauss. I will now have to clean up the mess that you have created. You should pray that I am successful."

Forbes about turned on his heels and marched out of the door with one final shout.

"Think about your position Planner."

John slammed his hands onto his desk and looked around the room in despair. What more could he do? He rubbed the bridge of his nose once more; he felt one hell of a migraine coming on. *Bugger it*! he thought. He walked over to his coat stand and put on his suit jacket and rain coat. He opened the door to the secretaries' area and marched past Laura's desk. "I'm off home Laura; I have had enough for one day. Bye."

Chapter 3 The University Dig

Professor Doug Baillie scratched his thinning scalp in frustration as he looked over the scanned images of mediaeval manuscripts and plans of the church his tent was pitched next to. The passage to the original crypt was not where it was supposed to be. He could understand there being some mistakes on the ancient plans but he knew there should still be some sign of the passage. They had been searching the lower corridor for a week now with no success and he was beginning to lose heart plus the students would be leaving in the next day or so for their Christmas break. He stretched feeling the bones in his back crack then jumped at the sound of excited voices outside his tent so he got up to investigate.

Kirsty Legget, a tall redhead in her early twenties who always set his heart racing, was jumping up and down whooping loudly at the entrance to the church. She saw Doug and shouted to him. "Professor we think we found the Vampire crypt! Come and see it."

Without waiting she raced back into the entrance of the church followed by Doug. He could feel his heart racing as they descended the stairs that led steeply down in a sharp left turning curve. The string of lights powered by the generator flickered randomly but Doug failed to notice this anymore. His mind was utterly focussed on the prospect of finding the fabled vampire's crypt.

It did not take long for them to reach the bottom of the stairwell and the lower corridor. Doug could always smell the dampness in the dirt walls before he saw the bottom of the stairs. He could hear the excited chatter of his students at the far end of the corridor. Three of the students, Lisa, Steven and Shaun were gathered around a hole in the wall. Shaun held a *Zippo* lighter up to the gap and Doug could see that the flame was flickering wildly. Shaun smiled and gave Doug a thumbs up.

Doug walked over to the hole and shone a torch into the gap; he could feel a cold damp draught on his face and couldn't help but smile. If he was correct then the draught came from an underground stream that separated the crypt from this corridor.

"Has anyone been through yet?" He asked.

"We wanted you to be first Professor." Shaun said and proffered a safety helmet that Doug put on. The others followed suit.

"No time like the present." Doug said and ducking his head, stepped into the damp, musty corridor followed by his students. Steven followed at the back the light from his video camera was pinpointed on the rest of his group.

The corridor gradually descended and turned slowly to the left so that the torch beam did not light all the way to the end. At first there was just the rumour of running water but as they walked further it grew in volume until there seemed to be a torrent of water somewhere in front of them. Doug felt confident they were on the right track now and advanced with determination. The wall of the tunnel was now slick to the touch with frozen moisture and Doug noticed that the floor now curved upwards at either side so that the tunnel formed a natural pipe through the rock. Their breath came out in great foggy clouds now illustrating how much the temperature had dropped. The tunnel finally opened out into a round natural chamber that was almost the size of a football field.

Approximately halfway across the chamber a wide stream raced along a channel frothing and bubbling in a crescendo that echoed off the walls so loud that Doug had to shout.

"The stream looks too wide to cross without some sort of aid but I think the remains will be buried across there if the legends are correct."

Steve used the zoom on his video camera to examine the area around the stream. He focussed in on what seemed to be a pile of rubble. He took a few seconds then shouted above the noise of the water.

"Professor I think there are some long stone slabs over in that pile of rubble to the left of the chamber." He used the light from the camera to highlight the rubble. Doug and Shaun moved across the chamber to the rubble followed by the others. Upon examining the pile Doug noticed that there were indeed three long lengths of what seemed to be granite covered by a small pile of loose rocks. The granite looked as though it had been placed there some time ago and the rocks had fallen from the ceiling over the years. Doug thought that someone had left the granite there on purpose, perhaps the soldiers that had been here in the Second World War. He felt it strange that it should be made so easy for them to access the burial chambers once they had managed to locate the correct passage. It was almost as if they were being given a helping hand. This thought vaguely disturbed him although he wasn't sure why but he dismissed it almost at once when he thought of the prestige of finding the legendary vampires of the Black Loch. He would finally be properly recognised for his work rather than being thought of as a crank. The university team worked together to lift the granite and over a series of runs managed to push all three into place so that they could now walk across a fairly wide footpath to the far side of the chamber without having to step into the icy water.

Doug led the way once more and strode towards the far wall where he could now make out the shape of a large cross. As he got nearer to the far wall Doug could see that the cross was actually separate from the wall. It was iron, he reckoned and around three feet in length and was set within an iron clip. On further investigation he noticed that the clip locked a small hidden door in the wall. The students gathered round him and he was conscious of Steven filming him. The cross unnerved him because it did not seem to be ancient. He felt certain that it could have been added as recently as sixty years before when the soldiers were here. He pondered what to do. He knew he had come too far and spent too much time on this research not to remove the cross, but somewhere deep in the innermost part of his mind a warning bell was ringing about doing this.

He shrugged and reaching forward removed the cross. A howling wind screamed along the channel of the stream and the entire group looked around the chamber. It seemed like a banshee had entered the place, screeched her way around them and then departed along the course of the water.

They heard a grinding sound and a large piece of stone gave way in the floor of the stream. The water plunged down through this and disappeared somewhere underground. Doug noticed that it no longer dissected the chamber now and there was now a safe path across the chamber on the right hand side. They all looked at one another, Kirsty stood slack jawed her mouth forming a silent o.

"What the hell was that?" Shaun asked, turning in a slow circle, Steven did the same, turning the camera a full 360 degrees.

"I'm not sure. Perhaps the air pressure changed when this little door opened or when the floor of the stream gave way." Doug said doubtfully.

Shaun cocked an eyebrow at his professor and Doug knew none of the students were convinced but they needed to go on. He actually felt a little frightened but he had to show confidence or panic would spread among them. He used the edge of the cross to prise the old door open a bit more, and soon there was enough space for them to enter the chamber behind it one at a time.

He shone the torch inside; the passage was only about fifteen feet long and ended at a broken burial chamber. Doug walked up to the cracked stone covering and ran his fingers along the strange carving on its surface. It was a strange hybrid of Celtic and Pictish that he had only seen a couple of times before. He felt certain that this was proof that he had found the legendary vampire's lair. He felt great tingles of excitement as he carefully lifted the pieces of the cover and put them to the side. "Bring the camera, Steven! I want to capture this."

Steven shook his head and pointed over Doug's shoulder.

What the hell? Confused, Doug turned round, then froze on the spot

He was face to face with a perversity of humanity - an obscenity and offence to everything that was decent on this earth. A vaguely humanoid face was inches from him but instead of looking into the eyes of a person he was staring into the abyss. Silver discs shone with an evil light of their own.

Even as it happened he knew that he was somehow being mesmerised. He now knew how a mouse must feel when a snake has it trapped. He wanted to run but his limbs refused to heed him. Another part of his mind turned traitor and told him to offer himself to the master. He would become one with a powerful force beyond his comprehension.

A cold presence seemed to crawl along his mind, its tendrils creeping into every nook and cranny as it explored his intellect. Yes the master would treat him well; his intelligence would be recognised and respected. For one small moment of pain followed by a bitter sweetness he could not imagine he would become powerful, a man apart. Doug wanted this; he waited patiently as the master crawled further forward. The huge mouth opened and the jaw seemed to unhinge at an impossible angle. A foul stench came from that ancient mouth surging past the yellowed razor sharp canine teeth. Doug let out a sigh as the mouth clamped on his neck. Shaun did not wait long enough to see all this he turned and ran back the way they had come.

"Get the fuck out of here!" He shouted. He banged into Steven almost knocking the forgotten camera from his hands. He didn't care about any of the rest of them; he wanted to save his life. All that women and children patter was good enough in films but when it came down to it Shaun was like most people and prized his life above others. He sprinted out across the chamber and raced for the recently made bridge across the stream.

He heard Kirsty scream but did not look back.

Kirsty had noticed movement above them at the last second just before the vaguely female figure dropped from the ceiling. She tried to run but the assailant grabbed her long her and yanked her head back. The end was mercifully quick. The creature slashed at her throat with its teeth but her head had been yanked back so viciously that her neck had broken and she was dead before the creature fed on her.

Lisa had remained further back than the others and when Steven ran past her she picked up the heavy cross and threw it at the female figure that stood over Kirsty's body. The creature let out a terrified screech and jumped up into the air clutching onto the roof of the passage. It started balefully at her but Lisa had seen how the other creature had mesmerised the professor and knew not stare back.

She ran for her life.

She crossed the now drying course where the fast running stream had flowed just behind Steven. She did not want to look back but very quickly realised they weren't going to escape.

The female creature had overtaken them by crawling along the ceiling with incredible speed and dropped just in front of them. With a rapid swipe she struck Steven across the head and threw him across the chamber. He collided with the far wall and slid to the floor lifeless.

Lisa tried to dodge to the side but the creature grabbed her and threw her back towards the passage. She slid on her back and was facing the way she was sliding. To her horror she saw that the first creature was on all fours facing her. A weird voice was in her head now and with a cold certainty she knew it was over.

The voice told her that she would enjoy living here in the twilight and not to fear the pain. As Doug had done, Lisa gave herself to the master. Her vision diminished and darkness came creeping in from all angles like a television screen that was being shut down. It overcame her and she knew nothing more.

The female creature and the master stared at one another for a second, a message seemed to flash between them and she turned back to the chamber to chase after Shaun.

Shaun could hear his own heartbeat pounding within his head as he puffed and panted for breath - but knew he could not afford to slow down. By the time Lisa was being set upon he had reached the pipe like tunnel and sprinted along it desperate not to lose his footing on the uneven ground.

He risked a glance over his shoulder and immediately regretted it.

The female creature was barrelling along the tunnel, racing on all fours in a feline surge. She was moving along the walls of the tunnel and over the ceiling before coming down the other side and starting the process over and over again as she closed the gap between them.

He quickly looked away when he realised that she was staring at him with those horrible silver disc eyes. He had seen what that did to the professor and did not want to suffer the same fate. He had reached the hole they had forced through the wall and ducked to go through, at that moment he made the last mistake of his life. He glanced back.

The creature tackled him in the way a lioness would take down a zebra. She hissed and spat at him, her long talons clawed deep into his ribs and her head thrashed left and right as she tried to rip his throat out with her teeth. The two of them rolled head over heels and crashed into the far wall with a dull thud. Shaun groaned with all the wind knocked out of him, he let out one last sigh as the razor sharp teeth bit into his throat. He could feel his strength flow out of him along with his life blood and the pain soon left him.

His last thought was that she had a severe case of dog breath.

Chapter 4 The Electric Compound

Steven Morrison visibly jumped as the compound buildings entrance was hit by something hard. He looked across at Barry Woolich who thumped down on the table.

"I'm sick of this." Barry snarled. "Put on the spotlights Steven we are going to tell these idiots that we have their car number and the police will be informed."

"Don't go out there Barry," Tom pleaded, "You know what young neds are like, they'll have knives. Kids don't care nowadays; at the very least they will annoy us for longer. Let's just go deeper into the compound, and then we won't hear them. They can't get over the fence anyway."

Barry shook his head. He pointed to the large tool chest against the wall. "I can take the bolt gun; it looks like a pump action shot gun. That ought to scare them off."

"Okay, but don't go outside to them. It isn't worth it."

"I won't." Barry walked over to the chest and picked out the gun while Steven pulled down the switch for the powerful spotlights. Steven followed Barry to the large heavy steel door and waited while the hydraulics opened it. They looked out across the open compound towards the bright lit gates. Just outside the light radius stood two figures. Barry thought they were a bit tall for the youths and couldn't see the Subaru car they drove. He walked slowly towards the gate bringing the gun up to the at arms position.

"Okay guys enough is enough," he shouted. "Fuck off back to your mum or I'll give you a whiff of shotgun. We've already called the police."

"Why would you threaten us Barry? We just want to be let inside."

Barry walked towards the gate faster, thinking that he recognised the voice. "Is that you, David? Where have you both been all day?" He felt a wave of relief wash over him and he lowered the bolt gun as he advanced.

Steven had followed Barry out when he realised it was his colleagues the other side of the fence. He watched from a distance.

The taller of the two figures walked into the light but remained a short distance from the gate. He inclined his head and spoke with a slight lisp in his voice. "We had an accident with the jeep. It slipped off the road in the rain we slid before smacking a tree. I think we were stunned. When we came to we walked back. Let us in Barry."

The other figure stepped forward and they both started chanting, ""Let us in Barry, let us in Barry, let us in Barry."

"Okay, okay!" Barry said. He dropped the bolt gun and stepped forward to open the gate.

Steven suddenly felt alarmed. It was something about the strange way they chanted. He picked up the discarded bolt gun and watched as Barry unlocked the gate. "Barry don't…" he began to say but it was too late, Barry had opened the gate and he heard him say.

"Come on in."

In that instant both of their colleagues jumped on top of Barry hauling him to the ground. They opened their mouths impossibly wide and bit down on his neck and belly.

Stephen was rooted to the spot, unable to believe what he was seeing.

"Help me!" Barry screamed. His petrified eyes pleaded with Steven.

Steven looked down at the bolt gun in his hands and saw that it was fully loaded with a 30 bolt clip. He aimed at David's back and fired three shots. The first ripped into David's back, the second his shoulder and the third missed. Barry's head fell back and his eyes rolled up into his head. Steven suspected he was dead and backed off towards the compound building as David looked up at him.

In the spotlights Steven could see that David's eyes were now silver reflective discs. He had no whites no iris just a silver disc.

David glanced over his shoulder at the two bolts sticking out of his back then looked at Steven. His mouth opened into a lupine grin and he hissed. "Why did you do that Steven? Don't you want to join us? I can make it almost painless...."

Steven suddenly knew he had to flee for the sake of his immortal soul.

"Go to hell!" He screamed. as he ran towards the building. He looked back when he reached the entrance and saw the strangest thing just before the hydraulic door slammed shut. David and Mark sprinted towards the gate and just as they were about to cross the small bridge over the burn at full speed they fell backwards. For all the world it looked as thought they ran into a glass wall. If Steven weren't so terrified he would have found it hilarious. He checked that the solid hydraulic steel door was locked and headed deeper into the compound; he closed and locked the next door. He stood with his back to the door, gasping to get his breath back, and desperately wondering what to do next. He looked around the office and saw the pc in the corner.

"E-*mail*!" He said aloud, running towards it. He switched on the pc and while it powered up he looked at the cctv screens. His heart quickened as he watched the two figures pacing outside the gate as if they were debating what to do, then they disappeared into the darkness. Steven hastily typed an email to head office; carefully wording it so that Police would arrive without thinking his story was completely nuts. He pressed 'send' on the computer and then sat back in the chair, unconsciously, running his hand absently along the crucifix hanging from his neck.

Chapter 5 The Post Office

The radio handset went off and Sergeant Tom McKillop nodded towards it.

WPC Claire Lawell stared at him as she reached for it. "What did your last slave die of Tom?"

"I'm driving, Claire; it is safer that you answer." He smiled.

A disembodied voice filled the Police jeep.

"Come in two six, we have received a call from Scottish Power that they received an email from a compound in the area you are visiting. They request that you check on the compound after you have visited the archaeological dig. Do you copy?"

"Roger that." Claire said winking at Tom.

"Knock that off Claire just visit the compound and radio in when you are there. We also have a report of four missing youths who were last known to be in the area. They were from the village of Cothqon on the other side of the mountain and were in a red 95 Subaru Impreza keeps your eyes open for that."

"Yes Inspector." Claire answered.

"Ok, well both of you be careful there is more snow predicted for the hills. Over and out."

Claire laughed and looked over at Tom.

"You know he hates that roger patter Claire."

"Yeah I know," She agreed.

Tom found it amusing having a young partner for a change. Claire was new out of Jackton and very keen but the new officers were different from his day. He was old school, but tried to keep an open mind and he found having someone young enough to be his daughter with him caused him to think of cases differently.

"Okay," he said, "here's the post office. Last stop before we leave civilisation." The smile on Claire's face turned to a frown as they drew to a halt outside the post office and the adjoining cottage. There were hawthorn decorations around all of the windows and along the door frame. Something about the hawthorn prodded at a memory in Claire's mind but she couldn't put her finger on it. She was about to mention it to Tom but he was already knocking on the door.

A small portly elderly man answered the door, he had old fashioned prince nez spectacles on that half hid lively brown eyes. A shock of grey hair surrounded a bald crown and he had a neatly trimmed beard. He gestured into the cottage and the police officers gladly went inside out of the cold mountain wind.

They all sat down at a wooden table and the old man offered them tea which they accepted.

Tom took a sip of the hot tea. "Mr Collins," he said, we were informed that you reported the uni students missing?"

"Call me Robert, son." the old man said. "Yes I did. I'm afraid two or maybe four Scottish Power workers might be missing too. There were two lads who would come down every evening to pick up their mail and to leave mail for going out. Yesterday and today they didn't turn up. Now I can accept one day but not two especially if you know the history of this area." He looked pointedly at Claire.

"Are you Hughie Lawell's daughter?"

"Yes," Claire told him.

"I was sorry to hear about your parents dear, too many accidents happen on the roads up here."

Claire nodded.

"However I think we all know that sometimes there are more than accidents in these hills."

Tom looked at Claire's poker face.

"What do you mean Mr .. eh Robert? I have heard there are crash black spots here but nothing else."

Robert raised an eyebrow "There are local tales of strange things happening to people up in these hills every few years. There will be a spate of so called road accidents with the bodies gone from the scene, a good few people will go missing things like that then things will go quiet for a few years. There will be families in the more remote parts who just seemingly leave overnight. Some are found to have left to escape debts that sort of thing but others are never heard of again. I know several families who have complained of noises in the night, people trying to climb in their windows, rattling the glass and demanding to get in. Farm animals being found dead drained of their blood. The list goes on and on."

Tom looked from Robert to Claire . "You are messing with me aren't you?" He said giving a goofy smile. "Both of you winding up the cop from the big city?" They both slowly shook their heads.

The smile slipped from Tom's face. "Okay, so what are we talking about here? You think there are vampires or zombies out in the hills?"

"Strange things have happened out in the hills. You can check back in the local papers if you don't believe me. All I know is we have been getting disturbed in recent nights with people knocking on the windows after dark and shouting for us to let them in. I can tell you something for nothing: it scares the hell out of me and the wife."

Robert took a sip from his tea and as he moved Claire noticed the large cross round his neck, she unconsciously felt for hers beneath her uniform.

"Okay," Tom conceded, "Let's just for a moment suppose that there is something strange in the mountains here. It is far more likely to be something like a man on the run from Carstairs hospital or something, than a monster out of a horror film. I can understand you feeling vulnerable in this remote area, sir, but I can assure you if there is someone attacking people we will get to the bottom of this."

"I didn't mean any offence, son," the old man said. "I am just trying to say, watch your back out there. I assume I can't talk you into waiting here till morning?"

Tom shook his head slowly. "I am sorry; sir but we are police officers. The moment we back off from something through fear then we lose authority, and if we lose authority we can't do our job. We have to visit the site of the dig and the Scottish power compound and discover what is going on. Surely you understand that Robert?"

Robert nodded his understanding, and he looked at Claire who briefly smiled. He cleared his throat and spoke softly with obvious embarrassment. "If you must go up there tonight then would you indulge a foolish old man and take these small gifts? I could not live with myself if I did not try to give you some protection."

He reached behind himself and opened a drawer in a mahogany sideboard; he produced two silver crosses on leather thongs and placed them on the table.

"Please wear these will you?"

Claire lifted one, and put the thong round her neck.

Tom hesitated.

As if reading his mind Robert said. "Humour an old man please."

Tom put the thong round his neck. He drummed at the table for a second then said.

"We really must be going."

The two police officers stood and Robert followed suit. They both shook hands with the old postmaster and left the post office. Robert bolted the door behind them in three places and walked through the house to a back bedroom. An old lady sat on the bed knitting.

"Did you manage to talk the police out of going to the mountains?" She asked.

"No, Mary. There was no point. They are Police, they need to go there. I gave them the crosses though."

"Will it be enough?"

"I don't think so but one of them was Hughie Lawell's daughter, so at least she is aware of the stories about the mountains that will give them a chance."

"I hope so Robbie. She was a lovely wee girl."

Chapter 6 Further Into the Mountains They Go

The jeep drove further into the mountains and Tom had to switch on the headlamps sooner than he had thought he would. The clouds were starting to descend from the mountain tops and they looked heavily pregnant with snowstorms. He tapped on the brakes as they reached a fork in the road. He glanced both ways then turned down the right hand fork. "We should see the loch in a few minutes. It's only 2 miles or so to where the dig should be." Claire said. Tom glanced at the jeep radio and noticed there was no signal on the front of it. He picked up the handset and clicked transmit a couple of times.

"Have you got a signal on your mobile Claire?"

She twisted in her seat and produced a tiny mobile phone from her jacket pocket. She stared at the screen on it and shook her head. "Not even emergency calls. What about yours?"

He gestured to the glove compartment so Claire opened it and brought out his bulky old mobile phone. She smiled at how out of date it was.

"What? Not hip enough for a young thing like you?"

She laughed a little and looked at the old green pixelated screen. "Nope - no signal on yours either. So we are incommunicado. Do you think we will get a signal at the loch?"

"I doubt it." Tom looked at the mountains that descended from either side and obviously came down to meet at the loch. "Those chunks of rock probably block out all transmissions. We might get a signal at the compound if it is higher up."

"Hmmm." Claire murmured doubtfully. She glanced up at the lowering clouds then at the road ahead of them.

"Maybe the compound has a secure landline." He offered.

"it's gonna be dark soon. I hope the snow doesn't get too bad. It could be difficult coming down from here if the weather closes in."

"We will be ok. I have driven jeeps most of my adult life."

"Ooh my hero." Claire teased. "Ok let's get to the dig and get this started so we can get back as soon as possible."

Tom put the foot down and accelerated along the road.

Very soon the vista opened out in front of them. Instead of the claustrophobic hedgerows and dry stone dykes they now so a wide expanse of dark freshwater. At the three other sides mountains rose up from the loch side while on the side they were at a pebble beach fell gradually away from them towards the water. They drove onto the beach and the pebbles crunched and slid out under the jeeps wheels as it drove steadily towards a short neat row of tents which had various accoutrements of camping strewn around them in haphazard piles. Tom pointed to a pile that looked as though it had been deliberately scattered. They drove around the far side of the tents and Claire noticed there were tyre tracks that preceded theirs and seemed reasonably fresh that led to and from the water side. Tom drew the jeep to a halt at the far end of the tents and climbed out followed by Claire. She loosened the catch on her truncheon instinctively; she noticed that Tom had done the same.

"Hello!" he shouted as he advanced on the first tent. He gestured to Claire to walk to the other side. They walked along the tents parallel to one another. The tents were set up so that the openings alternated on either side, the first opened on the waterfront the second facing the land the third on the waterfront and so on. Tom looked in the first tent and saw that it was empty. He stood back up and shook his head at Claire. She looked in the second. It was empty except for socks and a pair of boots that were abandoned carelessly. She looked across at Tom and shook her head.

Tom headed to the third tent and froze when he looked inside. "Claire …" he called in a hoarse, shocked voice.

"What is it?" Claire ran down the narrow alley between the second and third tents. Tom was holding the flaps of the tent open. He swallowed hard and gestured inside with a nod of his head. "Jesus! It looks like our worries about the uni team were right."

Claire squeezed in beside him to see better.

The interior of the tent skin was matted black. There were clotted clumps of something attached to the skin at various points and the tent stank of death and decay. Claire put a hand to her nose and mouth and spoke in a muffled voice. "Is that … is that blood?"

"I think so." Tom said, "And if I'm right those clumps are pieces of flesh and skin. Something or someone was torn to pieces inside here. "God almighty!" He stepped back from the tent and let the flaps fall back to cover the tent.

Claire quickly followed him. "We better call this in Tom." She pulled out her mobile phone and saw it still had no signal. She was about to run back to the jeep when Tom grabbed her wrist firmly.

"We will drive to get a signal but we need to check that there is no one lying here hurt first. Come on let's quickly check the tents but be very careful." He withdrew his truncheon. Claire took a deep breath then did the same.

"Ok, Let's do this." She said. She was still shocked at what they had found but was determined to show she had what was needed from a police officer. She headed back to her previous position and they continued their search.

After a few minutes they ascertained that three of the tents had been the sites of horrific attacks but the others were untouched. What puzzled Tom the most was the lack of other evidence. There should have been rips to the tents or signs of a body being dragged along the beach. He supposed they could have been dumped in the water and then the pebbles brushed but something or someone that committed such savagery surely did not care about covering their tracks. Did they? He looked up and down the beach, confused. He jumped as Claire tapped his arm.

"This doesn't look good for the compound either does it?"

Tom could see that the colour had drained from her face. He glanced again at the beach. "I think we should head back to the jeep. We need to make sure we don't contaminate the scene any further than it already is. We will go up to the compound and see what the situation is there. Hopefully there will be a phone line and we can call for back up and Scene of Crime Officers. I know how shocking this all is Claire but we are the officers on scene so we need to check everything out. Okay?"

"Yes, I understand." Claire said. She was very uncomfortable with the carnage she had seen but was even more determined to show Tom that she was capable and in control. No matter how hard she tried though she could not get rid of the feeling that something more than an escaped psycho had carried out the horrors in the tents. She gave herself a mental shake and said. "Don't worry Tom, I can handle this. It's shocking ... but I think we need to keep our minds open on what did this so we don't get caught by surprise."

Tom looked hard at her. He knew Claire had done research on this area for her thesis at university and he would discuss this with her later. They might discover something that would help them.

"Okay, we will drive up to the compound but I want to quiz you a little on the way up. I think it might help us."

"Fine by me." Claire said and climbed in the jeep.

Tom started the engine. He turned the vehicle and drove back along the road.

"Okay Claire, you did research on the local stories here and tried to relate it to actual cases here didn't you?"

"Yeah, there is a crazy amount of people have gone missing in these mountains over the years. Like Robert said families would buy or rent houses then vanish overnight. Some were traced and found to be running away from debt collectors, sometimes husbands ran out on their wives etc but there were many that had no explanations. I focussed on cases that the Police investigated and it was like something from the X files." She paused clearly looking for a good example. "Okay, the one that will convince you is the case of Lucy Steadman. She was a bit of a girl and went missing in 1978. I think it was with one of her boyfriends when she was 17. Anyway when she didn't return the next morning her mum called the police and a full scale search took place. The mountain rescue was involved too along with the RAF helicopters. It was a small team including Sergeant Davie Dunlop that found her. They found the car first smashed into a tree further along the loch the boyfriend was inside it his neck broken in the crash. That was the days before 'clunk click before every trip'. They searched around the car for a while then found Lucy a short distance away hanging from a tree by her feet. Her head had been removed and placed on the ground below her. I spoke with Sergeant Dunlop at the old folk's home as part of my dissertation research. He made me swear not to print this next part as they had been told to be quiet about it - but he told me that there was not a single drop of blood in her body and there were only a few small splatters below her. There should have been pints and pints of it."

Tom thought about this for a second. Davie Dunlop was a legend in the force, he had lead a lot of murder investigations when he was in CID and was known for his no nonsense approach to police work. Davie would not make up something like that.

"Who told him to keep quiet about it - his senior officers?"

"No, he said they were met by some soldiers they thought were helping the search and the chief inspector was there with some sort of senior military officer there. He had no unit badges on him neither did any of the other soldiers. It was the army officer who told him then left with his men to go to the crime scene. The chief inspector then insinuated if he wanted a good career in the Police he had better keep quiet about the details. The official story would be they were killed in a car crash. Doesn't it strike you as weird that the army took over the crime scene?"

None of this made sense to Tom. The army had no right doing that and he couldn't understand why a senior police officer would give in to an army officer. "Okay, the only thing I can think of is that they must have been some sort of specialist security team. Ignoring that for a second - the murder of Lucy doesn't fit the modus operandi here. The tents looked as though people had been ripped apart inside them while Lucy's body was drained. If it were some sort of vampire type creature then surely all the blood would be gone, would it not?"

"Are you mocking me, Tom?" Claire raised her eyebrows.

"No. I'm just keeping an open mind here, and trying to look at things methodically. If there are killings going on throughout the years that are linked somehow, then would they not follow a similar pattern?"

"Stick with me on this please, Tom. I spent time investigating a number of the killings for my dissertation. There is a definite pattern. There seemed to be three distinct types." She had his attention now. "The first was like Lucy where the head would be removed and the body would almost be completely devoid of blood, the second would be similar to the tents where bodies would be ripped to pieces in a display of savagery and the third type the people simply vanished. Not long after the people vanished their relatives would complain of visits in the night from them."

Tom rolled his eyes. "Now that sounds more like a movie vampire."

"*Now* you are mocking me."

"Only a little Claire, but the last explanation would be familiar to most people." Claire continued. "You can imagine the reaction of investigating officers to that. At the very least they would think the relatives were suffering from shock. The problem was that sometimes the family of the missing people would vanish within a few days too. And then their bodies would be found in a similar condition to the first two types or they would vanish completely. This leads me to the most interesting thing that Sergeant Dunlop told me."

"Which was?"

"That Lucy Steadman wasn't the only girl missing. She went out that night with a friend called Vicky Hart from Cothqon. They searched everywhere but never found Vicky's body. Sergeant Dunlop went out the next day to pay a visit to Vicky's parents in Cothqon but found just the father there in a distraught state. He said that Vicky had paid a visit the night before and asked to be let in but there was something wrong with her, something terribly wrong. He said he felt terrified of her. He shouted that she couldn't come into the house, but his wife argued and eventually Vicky asked them to come out and join her. His wife went outside and he hadn't seen her since. A few days later John Steadman connected a hosepipe to his exhaust pipe and died of exhaust fumes in a lock up garage. Around the same time the body of his wife Doris was discovered ripped apart in the woods behind their house."

"Jesus!" Tom was taking it seriously now, "How many murders have there been in these hills?"

"The best estimate I could give from my research is around about thirty but that is only since the 1950s. "

"But surely there would have been investigations?"

"There seem to have been investigations started but they always stopped suddenly. Interesting enough the army has been involved in several of these investigations."

"But why would the army be interested in these killings?"

"Maybe they see the potential of a biological weapon or something? A vampire would be a very deadly soldier."

Tom smiled at this. "I can't picture Count Dracula in camouflage gear. Can you?" She raised her eyebrows. "All joking aside, I think we should take some of the folklore seriously to try and protect ourselves. I know the chances of the killers being actual vampires are just about nil, but it does no harm to cover all the bases does it?"

"Ok, Claire well we have the cross side of things covered. Can't see us finding holy water or garlic up here."

"Maybe we'll be ok in sunlight but not when it's dark. The stories I researched and what Mr Collins down at the Post Office said, tally with the idea that they need to be invited into a building. I also read somewhere that they can't cross running water either so these points might give us a chance if we do get attacked. It does seem as though piercing the heart and removing the head from the body kills them."

Tom stared past her at the road ahead. He couldn't tell if Claire was joking or getting excited and forgetting her Police training, but it would do no harm to note the points she made.

"Claire, you don't really believe that there are real live blood drinking vampires roaming these hills do you?"

"Undead."

"What?"

Claire grinned. "Vampires are *undead*."

"Ha ha very good. Well you don't believe there are undead roaming these hills?"

"I doubt it very much, but there is definitely something weird about this area and we should keep our eyes peeled. The last thing I want is to get caught cold because I refuse to believe something is possible."

"Okay - let's check out the compound." His rubbed his neck with his hand as though there was some tension there, and then moved it back to the steering wheel. The jeep took a sharp right turn and with a spurt of gravel the jeep accelerated up the hill into the forest towards the Scottish Power compound.

It was fully dark now and Claire struggled not to shudder as the ancient woodlands crowded in around the forestry road. She looked out the side window but could see no further than a couple of feet beyond the first trees. It was easy to imagine some form of primeval predators racing through the trees parallel to their jeep keeping track of them just waiting for the chance to pounce. She forced herself to look away and then she noticed the lights ahead of them off to the left of the road. She took a deep breath. "That looks like our destination,"

****

The compound looked strangely out of place in the ancient forest. It resembled some exploratory space craft that had come from the furthest reaches of the galaxy and embedded itself into the hillside. The heavy duty portakabins were heavily armoured and had steel plate shutters over the windows. There were large bulkhead lights along the sides of these buildings and set high up in solid steel posts that cast out huge pools of bright white light from their shuttered lamps. The compound had a cleared car park with room enough for half a dozen vehicles. All of this was protected by a three metre high steel palisade fence. The only entrance through this was a gate accessed by a short steel plank bridge over a fast flowing stream. Tom slowed down as they approached this and edged the jeep across the bridge, the metal planks clanging as they drove over. He turned the jeep so that the rear faced the main entrance of the buildings and front faced back towards the gate.

"Are you ready Claire?" Tom asked, loosening his truncheon.

Claire did the same. "Yes...." She tried to sound calm but her heart was racing. They both got out the jeep and made their way to the building entrance. Tom made a point of remote locking the jeep, he wanted some sort of warning if someone tried to attack the vehicle. He did not fancy being stranded here overnight. All the talk of vampires was grating at his nerves now. He glanced nervously from side to side as they walked up to the armoured front door of the compound buildings. He didn't want Claire to see how jumpy he felt.

Claire looked around the door for an obvious sign of communicating with the people inside. Tom pointed to a flat panel set in the right hand side that had a paddle button it. She pressed this and there was a hiss of static then silence. Claire cleared her throat. "This is the Police, we were asked to check on the occupants of the Scottish Power Compound. Is anyone there?"

There followed a loud hiss that stopped abruptly and the door hinged slowly out towards them. Both officers stepped aside until the door opened then entered a brightly lit vestibule that reminded Tom of the airlocks in spaceships from his favourite science fiction movies. They both stepped over the lip of the doorway and climbed into the building. The door closed softly behind them. Another steel door opened to their left and they came face to face with a tall gangly middle aged man who aimed what seemed to be a shotgun directly at them. The man then lowered the gun and looked sheepish.

"I'm sorry, officers," he said, shaking his head. "but you can't be too careful out here. I'm Steven Morrison. I'm the manager here and I sent the e-mail looking for help." He held the gun up. "it's a bolt gun; I had to be sure you were not changed like my colleagues. I was pretty convinced when you came across the gate bridge but I needed to be sure so I let you enter the building yourself."

Claire threw an anxious glance at Tom.

"You know about this?" He gestured all around him then placed the mean looking bolt gun on the floor." Follow me, please."

They followed him further into the building.

As they went back through the door he had opened, Steven then quickly closed and locked it. He walked along a series of warren like corridors and finally brought them to a cosily lit room deep within the compound. It looked like a staff canteen with bedrooms leading off from it.

Tom and Claire sat down on padded benches that surrounded a Formica topped table. Steven went towards a large urn "Would you like some tea? You'll probably need it to warm you up." He tapped the side of it with a finger to check it was hot enough.

They looked at each other and shrugged.

"I suppose it wouldn't do us any harm," Tom said. He stuck his hand out, "I'm Tom ... and this is Clare ...."

"Well, officers, I'm glad you're both here." Steven went over to a cupboard and produced three mugs. He poured the tea and brought them over to the table along with sachets of UHT milk and sugar

Steven sat drinking his black and unsweetened tea as they emptied the contents of the sachets into their mugs. "I'm grateful that you came here. Were you told about my three missing colleagues?"

Tom nodded as he took a first sip of tea. "We were radioed as we were heading up here. We were checking on the university students at the archaeological dig site"

"There were four of us stationed here," Steven explained. "We're all specialists in setting up the lines and masts for wind turbines. We're normally sent in at early doors to make sure everything is ready for the preliminary works starting. We're well used to things like visits from local neds and that was what we were experiencing here at first." He gestured around the room. That's why we have the high fences and all the heavy duty portakabins. Thank God we had them." He shrugged.

"We had some of the local neds come along the last couple of nights throwing beer cans, calling us queers, daring us to come out and fight them - the usual drunken rubbish. At first we thought that was all we would face here." He suddenly stopped and put his head in his hands.

"Excuse me …" He was clearly upset now. "I need to get something stronger before I even speak about this."

He got up from the table and went out of the mess room and into a room just off the corridor. After a couple of minutes he reappeared with an unopened bottle of whisky. He broke the cap seal and then held the bottle out. "Would either of you like a drop?"

"We could do with it," Tom told him, "but unfortunately we're on duty. You go ahead."

The manager's hand was shaking as he poured the whisky into his tea. He took a long gulp, paused and then took another one.

"Look," he said, setting the mug down. "I don't know where to start here … I'm worried that you'll think I'm nuts." He shook his head. "I know what I saw though."

Tom laid his hands flat on the table.

"Steven, we need to find out what is happening here. My job is to deal with the facts so please tell us everything you saw, no matter how trivial or silly it may seem.

Steven looked from Tom to Claire then back to Tom again, and then he took another drink.

"Ok. There were four of us here. Myself, Barry Woolich, David Barrymore and Mark Walton. David and Mark would go down to the post office every day to send off hard copies of the daily reports from the site and to pick up any mail for us at the site. They would do this around three o'clock to catch the last mail and then come back and we would all have our dinner before shutting down the compound for the night. Two nights ago, they never came back at their usual time. By the time it turned eight pm and they had not returned, we decided Barry and me that we should shut up shop in case we got a visit from the local neds. We didn't want them being able to damage any of the equipment in here. We knew that we could watch the site entrance through the CCTV cameras and the lights would catch the arrival of the other two if they returned that night. Of course they didn't come back but we did get a visit from the local neds. Barry wanted to go out and challenge them but I talked him out of it. They tend to carry knives nowadays so I didn't fancy it getting violent on us. The next morning we radioed our base that the other two members of our team had not returned and we were worried about them. The person at head office said they would inform the police and asked us to get on with setting up here so we had a full day's work ahead of us. Before we knew it we were back here and it was dark again." Steven took another swig from his alcohol fuelled tea. His eyes swivelled nervously to either officer.

Claire had a horrible feeling that she knew exactly where this story was going. "We got a visit from the neds again about half nine but they only stayed a couple of minutes, threw something at the building and then left. Barry was furious and wanted to have a go at them. I only managed to talk him out of it by pointing out that the neds had left. About an hour later we heard something being thrown at the roof of the entrance again. Barry decided to take the bolt gun you saw out and to face them off. I went out with him but instead of the fat lad and his pals who had been annoying us earlier it was David and Mark standing just the other side of the little bridge. Barry ran out to open the gate for them. They claimed they crashed their jeep down the track on the way to the post office. You didn't happen to see it did you? It was an old Scottish Power Land Rover with a yellow light on the top." Tom and Claire shook their heads.

Steven slumped a little. "They said they must have been unconscious for a full day from the crash and needed help. The thing that alarmed me in hindsight was that they chanted, 'Let us in!' over and over again in a weird manner, it was so creepy. I tried to warn Barry that something was wrong but he opened the gate and said for them to come on in. The instant he did this they attacked him. David was actually biting at his throat and chest. I used the bolt gun on him but he still came at me. David's eyes weren't normal … they seemed like they were made of a silvery metal. I know how that sounds bizarre but it wasn't the moon or the bulkhead lights reflecting in his eyes. I turned and ran for the entrance to here. As I got to the doorway I looked back and saw the strangest thing. They were both racing after me and were crossing the bridge when they fell backwards as if they had hit an invisible clothes rope at neck height."

Claire started at this as she remembered the stream underneath the small bridge.

"Does the stream we crossed go all round the compound?"

"it does," Steven confirmed. "We're actually sitting on a small island. We picked the site deliberately for that reason. It is a small treeless island formed by a break in the stream and it rejoins itself just further downstream."

"Running water." Claire said.

"Neither of you seem to be surprised by my story," Steven said. "I expected you to think I was totally bonkers. I don't know whether to be relieved or really worried now." He finished his drink with a gulp and walked over to the urn. "More tea?"

"We've seen some strange things ourselves this evening," Tom said, rolling his eyes, "so we're not so freaked out by your story. We need to work out what we're going to do, but first - do you have any communication systems left here so we can call in to our base? Our radios and mobile phones aren't working."

"The only form of comms I have is email. We didn't have a phone landline as we thought the mobiles would work here. We do have broadband and it is buried deep so we shouldn't lose the connection It's in the office if you want to follow me."

Steven led the officers back through the labyrinthine structure to a small neat office filled with electronic equipment. There were screens for the CCTV cameras, several electric switches, lots of equipment that neither office recognised but one piece that they did. In the corner sat a typical workstation with a black box of a PC with the screensaver showing a Scottish Power symbol spinning around.

Tom sat down at the PC workstation and watched as Steven typed in the password to access the computer and then clicked open the email programme on the PC. "There you go, Tom, just leave it when you finish and it will go on to screensaver." He turned to Claire." Would you like to get something to eat? I can only offer microwave meals for you both but I am good at nuking them."

"Yeah, ok," Claire laughed, she looked over at Tom. "He'll eat anything that isn't healthy."

"Oh I have lots of choice for you then. We will wait for you in the mess, Tom."

****

When the other two left Tom typed in the general email address for their Inspector at the police station and sat thinking for a second. What could he write in the email that would not sound crazy? Eventually he decided to stick to the facts on what they had found and what they had been told by Steven. His short message detailed the carnage at the archaeological dig and requested for Scene of Crime

Officers and CID to be sent to the site. He signed off and then decided to do a little internet research on the area.

He did a quick Google search and was surprised to see there were hundreds of sites for Cothqon. He flicked through a few of them and saw lots of references to folklore in the area especially related to stories of vampires and similar types of incidents. He read in more detail about the history of the area and found that there were legends concerning vampire type creatures in the middle ages and that the Romans had even recorded being plagued by some sort of demons that drained them of their blood. The consistency of the legends interested Tom but he still didn't believe in the supernatural.

The final entry on the first page interested him greatly. The report on the website was written by an unnamed world war two researcher who claimed he interviewed a dying man who confessed that he had been part of a secret in Britain's darkest hour. It seemed that in 1940 a Captain Jim Dunlop led a specialist army unit that carried out experiments in raising a demonic creature or creatures in a now vanished village called Deil that was on the shore of the Black Loch somewhere. Tom read more into this realising that the officer could be relative of the famous Police Sergeant. According to the death bed confession the troops were part of a special occult bureau set up by British Intelligence to investigate any paranormal weapons that could be used against the seemingly invincible Nazis. Captain Dunlop was a specialist in Ancient Scottish History and Folklore at the University of Glasgow. He had quickly risen in the Occult Bureau to command a specialist unit that carried out experiments on sites reputed to be of occult importance. The village of Deil came to their notice due to the legends of vampire like creatures so they set up camp in the area after moving the villagers out. The troops in this unit carried out the sacrifice of a lamb in the village and there was a strange blood ritual where several of the men cut their hands and let the blood drip down a stone funnel into a crypt. The idea seemed to be to summon some sort of demon to make the land a death-trap for the Germans who threatened to invade and not surprisingly the plan went wrong. It seemed something did rise from the crypt but the men began to be killed off one by one. The researcher did not seem to know what happened after this he hinted that perhaps Captain Dunlop, who among his other skills was an explosives expert, may have blown up a nearby dam but the end result was that the village was drowned. Tom was startled by a double ding ringing noise then realised it would be the microwave. He closed down the internet browser then saw that he had an email message.

The message read short and simple.

Tom

We were concerned when we couldn't contact you. Thanks for confirming comms are down. Severe weather warning heavy snow headed your way. Would suggest batten down for night and attempt return in daylight. Reports of many missing people in Cothqon, Request that you drive by then head back to base to report before getting some well earned rest.

Paul

Tom read the message a couple of times, Inspector Paul Teale was known for the brevity of his messages. Tom looked at the CCTV monitors and saw that there was a blizzard outside. He hurried through to the mess to let Claire and Steven know the good news.

Claire was tucking into microwave spaghetti Bolognese, she looked up as Tom entered and he was amused to see a strand of spaghetti and some tomato sauce were stuck to her cheek. Steven gestured to an open cupboard piled high with ready meals. "Take your pick."

Tom glanced at the meals then sat on the edge of a table. "I'll take you up on that offer in a moment Steven. We are going to need to impose ourselves upon you tonight. I got an email from our station telling me that a snowstorm is in its way to here. We have been instructed to batten down for the night and then try and return in the morning when the storm passes."

Steven visibly relaxed at this news but Claire looked anxious. She picked at her spaghetti now rather than wolfing it down. She placed her fork down and then looked hard at Tom. "Did the message say anything else?"

Tom did not want to discuss the content in front of Steven so he shrugged and continued.

"Just an apology that we would be working beyond our shift time."

Steven clapped his hands together once and interrupted. "Ok I will show you where you can sleep. I would strongly advise that we keep in rooms next to one another and that no-one leaves the building on their own. I think we should be perfectly safe in here so long as we don't let anyone in we're not one hundred percent about."

"Do you have any shovels here Steven? We might need to dig the jeep out tomorrow. Should we lock the gates?"

"We have spades and other tools next to the comms room and the gate should be okay. For whatever reason they don't seem to want to cross the entrance so I cant see them all of a sudden changing what they do."

"Should we take turns at being on guard?" She asked now. "You know … in case we get visitors in the night?"

Tom looked at Steven. "Is the compound alarmed? Would we be able to sleep knowing that alarms would let us know if someone approached?"

Steven scratched his stubbly cheeks. "Yes the compound is fully alarmed. There is an alarm built into the fence and there is an infra red trip alarm across the open gateway. That was why I knew you were approaching. There are also some sensors set out on the roofs of the buildings and within the compound car park so we should be fine. I have the alarms set to very loud and have managed to sleep through the last couple of nights."

"I think we sleep in our clothes though ready to react to anything quickly. Steven is there any weapons here either legal or illegal? Don't worry we won't hold it against you if you have an unlicensed shotgun, I think that will be the last thing we need to worry about tonight."

Steven slowly shook his head.

"I don't have anything here. The best weapons we have are the bolt guns and there are some axes among the tools."

He thought for a second then continued.

"If these people or things attacking people are like vampires we might need to use more traditional weapons like sharpened sticks. Perhaps we can use the handles of some of the tools plus we have a large supply of wooden fence stakes for staking out plots of land and running wire between them."

"There are no such things as vampires'!" Tom was exasperated now. "I am sorry for shouting guys but there are no such things as vampires. Maybe we have some sort of cult acting here that thinks they are vampires but it is impossible for such creatures to exist. However, we don't know how many people are out there and we have to assume they will not back off just because there are police officers here." He shrugged. "But as you have said Steven it looks as though they can't force their way into here, so hopefully we can get through tonight and then get back to civilisation. Steven you will come with us in the morning."

Having sorted the plan out, Tom went over to the cupboard to pick his dinner for the evening.

Steven poured himself and Claire mugs of tea from the urn "I will give you some privacy just now while I work out which bedrooms we should use."

After Steven left Claire whispered. "What else did the email say?"

"We need to check Cothqon in the morning. It seems that most of the village are reported missing. We have then to head back to the Station and sign off for some rest."

Claire sipped her tea. "Do you think that many of the people from the village have been killed like the people at the dig?" .

"I don't know. The thing is - for all the evidence of deaths, we haven't actually seen a body yet."

"Come on Tom you saw the amount of matted blood and bits of flesh. No one could have survived that happening to them."

Tom held his hands in surrender "I know that but it might not have been human remains. I think it was but if we go strictly by the facts then we have no concrete evidence yet of murder. I am still keeping an open mind though so that we won't get sucker punched by people attacking us. We will check out Cothqon in the morning but it will be a quick drive round. If we see no evidence of life then we get the hell out of dodge. It is something for our replacements to check out. Does that sound better to you?"

"Assuming the jeep is ok and they let us leave."

Tom decided not to push the point with her. He found a pack of shepherd's pie and put it in the microwave. "So what about Steven's story? Do you believe him?"

"I think so. It fits with the previous history of here."

"Yeah but he could have checked it out online and given himself a yarn to tell."

"Why would he lie to us though?"

"I don't know. Maybe he had a fall out with his colleagues over something and murdered them."

"Now who is unbelievable?" Claire mocked gently.

Tom ran a hand through his thick curly hair. "I don't know Claire. I am just trying to make sense of things here. Vampires can not exist, that is madness. We should make sure we keep an eye on Steven tonight and try not to sleep too deeply"

"Don't think I will be able to sleep much tonight." Claire muttered into her mug.

Tom said nothing. He knew he wouldn't get sleep much either.

Steven showed the two police officers to rooms that connected to one another via a short inner corridor. Tom was surprised to see that the small single beds looked comfortable.

Steven gave them a short tour of one of the rooms explaining that the rooms were all the same.

"They're a bit cramped I am afraid but as you can feel they are pretty warm and the beds are comfortable. These are set in the area of the compound furthest from the outside so I have felt very safe sleeping in the room down there."

Steven pointed to a doorway just round the corner. "Unfortunately we need to share the shower next to my room, but there are a couple of toilets just beyond the shower. There are speakers for the alarm system in every corner so we should hear if there are any intruders in the compound. It's very basic but at least it is clean and comfortable."

Claire sat down on the bed and liked how comfortable it was.

Steven looked around. "I'll let you settle in. I am going to check on the alarm system once more then I will get some shut eye. I take it you will want to leave as soon as It is light?"

"Yes." Tom agreed, "We want to get back to Dumfries as soon as possible. If you have anything you really want to take with you then you should pack it." Steven nodded and headed back to the comms room. Claire sat down on the bed in her room. Through the connecting corridor she could see Tom and was within earshot. She bounced a little on the bed smiling to herself.

"It's almost like a slumber party except we don't have our pjs."

"Just don't be chapping on my door saying you are afraid of the dark Claire."

"Yeah right," she said, laughing – "as if!"

Tom looked thoughtful. "I think we should keep the bedroom doors open so that no one of us is closed off from the others. We don't want to get separated too much when we don't know the situation."

"Yeah could be an eventful night. I think Steven is right though this place seems really solid. They would need the strength of superman to force their way through all of that steel."

Tom lowered his voice.

"Yes but what if someone was to let them in?"

Claire pushed her head forward and looked down the corridor that Steven had walked down.

"You don't think he would do you?"

Tom shrugged, he genuinely didn't know but wasn't willing to take the risk. "I will check the comms room once Steven heads to bed. As far as I can tell the only way to the comms room from his bedroom passes here so if it is secure at that point then we should be ok."

Claire chewed her lip thoughtfully. "I don't think we should sleep."

"We will do it in shifts, one of us keeping watch but if you hear anything when it is your turn wake me up."

"Ok but you do the same with me."

"Deal."

They heard footsteps coming along the corridor and a second later Steven appeared.

He carried out a theatrical stretch and yawn. "Well I am going to bed for the night, I will have a bag packed ready to go first thing. I will set my alarm clock for 6 am as we won't be able to tell from in here when it is daylight without checking the cctv screens. Good night."

Both officers bid Steven good night as he walked away along the corridor to his bedroom. Tom watched him go and heard the door to Steven's room open but not close. That was good; Steven had remembered that none of them was to close their doors. Tom stretched his neck and said. "If you want to have a sleep first I will keep watch in the comms room?"

"Uh uh," Claire shook her head, "I would rather keep watch first, you drove all the way here so you probably need the early sleep more than I do plus you will be driving us out of here."

"Ok no arguments from me. Come on and check the comms and alarm with me and then you can make yourself comfortable."

"Lucky me." Muttered Claire as she followed Tom along the corridor.

Tom checked the alarm sensors and they were all signalling that they were working fine. Claire went off and made herself a strong mug of tea and came back to the comms room settling down in the leather office chair in front of the cctv screens.

Tom pointed to the screens indicating the power of the alarm sensors and described how they worked to Claire.

"How do you know this kind of thing Tom?" She took a sip from the mug.

"They are similar to sensors we used when I was in the military police. If my guess is right the cctv will immediately switch to show which sensor has been set off so you should see if it is an animal or a person. If that happens we will come running through because the alarms should be able to wake the dead."

"Claire, no matter what do not investigate anything on your own," he said solemnly. "I know you want to prove yourself. I was in your position once too but do not go out on your own and if you hear someone in here the same applies. Come and get me, I want you to promise me you will."

"I promise Tom. Don't worry, I have no intention of getting myself killed through being stupid."

"Okay. I will do the same when it's my turn to keep watch."

He looked at the screens once more and patted Claire on the shoulder. "Give me a shout at one am and I will relieve you. Keep alert."

"Don't worry, I'm too wound up to sleep."

After he left, Claire took a long sip from the mug, she took one look at the screens outside and saw that the blizzard was in full force still. She then turned to the pc and clicked onto the internet. She clicked on the browser history and smiled as she quietly read out some of the websites visited recently.

"Blonde babes take on brunettes – sounds interesting ha." She paused though when she saw that some news articles had been examined. She read through these and then clicked onto the site about the experiments in the second world war. She began to chew on the nail of her index finger, a habit she had from childhood when worried. She followed a few links from this original story until she arrived at a site dedicated to local legends.

The site made interesting reading. The area around the Black Loch had been described by the Romans as being an area where the local tribes carried out human sacrifices offering up prisoners of war to creatures in the loch. The tribes believed the creatures were imprisoned by the water and were always trying to escape, the offering of sacrifices was meant as a form of appeasement to these creatures they worshiped as Gods. It seemed that as long as the creatures were fed with the blood of victims then they remained where they were.

The site then raced forward several hundreds of years to the time of the Scottish wars of independence when English armies marched through the hills raping and pillaging in their attempts to subjugate the Scottish people. There were several records of English units burning down villages in revenge for the disappearance of armed patrols. Sometimes the bodies of the soldiers were found and there were descriptions of them being either drained of blood with their heads removed or there being chunks of flesh and cloth left behind.

Claire then flicked forward to the paragraphs relating to the second world war. Again there was the name of an army officer named Dunlop who was in charge on the site. Rumours had spread that before the villagers were evacuated some of them had seen the soldiers bringing in lambs and opening up an old church crypt. Some of the older villagers including the minister and the priest reported that the particular church crypt had a sealed iron trap door with a silver cross inlaid into it that led down to an underground pool. No one was sure of the significance of the pool but they all agreed that it was a place that had been commonly accepted as off limits. The minister in particular reported that he had argued with the officer in charge when he realised the soldiers were opening the trap door. He and the priest claimed they were frog marched out to a truck and driven out of the village never to return. Funnily enough it did seem that there was some sort of accident or sabotage at a nearby dam that drowned the village while some of the soldiers survived.

Claire decided to do a search online for Deil. She ran down through the listings and clicked on a backdated article in the Glasgow Herald about the village of Deil being flooded in 1940. The report was short but stated that a dam had collapsed in an area near the black loch drowning an old village of weavers cottages. Fortunately the army had managed to evacuate the village earlier in the month as the land was needed for military training according to the article.

Claire then looked at another backdated article in the Scotsman that referred to villagers from the village of Deil complaining that the government had not helped them find permanent accommodation after their village was evacuated. There were references to lawyers considering taking the Government to court. A government spokesman had made a bland statement to the effect that the villagers had all been adequately compensated. The very matter of fact way that the stories were reported gave corroboration in Claire's mind to the legend of the village. She then decided to do a search on Captain Jim Dunlop. Most of the listings referred to articles she had already looked at but one was an obituary from just a few years before. She clicked on it and saw a photograph of a handsome if thin young man in army uniform. She read the article but it was very bland telling mainly of an officer who served in the ranks of British army intelligence before going onto a career in the foreign office then spending his final years before retirement as a history professor at the University of Glasgow. Claire wondered about that. Was it a coincidence that the archaeology team at the dig were from the same University. She made a note of that in her pocket notebook and then decided to check out some entertainment so she clicked on *Youtube*. She still had some time to kill.

****

Tom jumped awake and suddenly realised the klaxon alarm was going off! Immediately he knew they were warning that the perimeter had been breached. He slammed his feet down on the floor and even through his sleep blurred vision he could see that Claire's bed was empty. He shouted above the din for Steven, but then he saw the manager was already running towards him.

"They must have broken the perimeter." Steven roared. Tom sprinted to keep up, concerned now about Claire's safety.

They turned the final corner to the comms room and saw it was empty. Steven looked at the screen and saw several figures standing just across the small bridge. Tom ran past the room towards the main entrance, he had a horrible feeling that was where Claire would be.

Tom saw that the entrance door was ajar and there were footprints visible in the snow within the small area that he could see. He pushed the door further open and ran out. Claire was kneeling at the side of the jeep, staring out at three figures standing on the other side of the gate and bridge.

"Let us in, let us in, let us in." They chanted over and over again in sibilant voices.

It gave Claire the creeps but she felt too frightened to move.

"Claire!!" She heard Tom calling, and she turned and saw him running towards her. He looked at her feet and saw she was kneeling beside a full grown deer. Its head was separated from the body; the corpse did not seem to have any blood within it. Tom looked at this for a second then returned his gaze to the three men at the gate. They stared intently back.

Tom felt that he was looking into the eyes of cold naked evil. The eyes of an emotionless killer. He was reminded of nature programmes about great white sharks. He was always amazed at how cold and calculating their eyes looked. He now felt as though he were one of those countless seals he had seen being torn apart by the ultimate predator. Tom had to force himself to look away but still the men chanted their demand for entry.

He whispered into Claire's ear. "When I nudge you we run for the building."

Claire nodded and when she felt his touch, they both sprinted for the doorway, ignoring the howls of the men behind them. They crossed the doorway and Steven was waiting on them. He hit the switch for the main door which slid shut behind them.

"Now do you believe me?" Asked Steven leaning with one arm against the top of the inner doorway.

"Get inside, we will close this door too," Clare panted. "I won't feel safe till we have done that."

Once the second door slid shut Tom said," I feel chilled to the bone. Why did you do that Claire? I told you to wake us if anything happened."

Claire looked at the ground.

"I don't know, I sort of wasn't myself. It was as though someone ordered me out and I obeyed them. Stupid of me."

"You need a hot drink," Steven told him. "We all need one – with plenty of whisky in them."

Chapter 7 Cothqon

The village of Cothqon had settled down for the night. Being a rural area in winter there were none of the late night activities you would see in a large town or city, everyone was hunkered down either in bed or sitting around their hearthside. No-one was outside to witness the eight figures that walked out of the forest and along the main road. The figures split up and headed off in different directions.

Becky Maxwell sat at the kitchen table nursing a lukewarm mug of tea. Her husband Callum strode up and down the kitchen; Every so often he ran a hand through his shoulder length hair.

"I swear to God Becky I will kill the boy for putting us through this once he comes home."

"Callum the police will find him soon. He might have had an accident or something." She drew on a cigarette, greedily inhaling the smoke begging for nicotine to calm her nerves. She looked warmly at her husband of twenty years. "I know you are worked up honey, just let the police do their job and don't jump to conclusions."

"Becky those boys he runs about with are bad news. If we don't stop this he might end up in the jail or worse." He leant over the table as if ready to say something else when the back door was knocked.

Callum walked to it and moved aside the axe onto the pile of firewood he had chopped earlier. He undid the three bolts on the door and came face to face with his son Ally. The security light he had fitted failed to come on so Ally's face was mainly in shadow and Callum could see he only had his light jacket on while standing in the blizzard outside. There was something strange but he could not work out what bothered him.

"Ally! What happened to you?" He exclaimed. Becky stood up and advanced to the door elated her son had returned to them.

"Let me in Dad, it's freezing out here."

"Of course you can come in." Becky exclaimed. Callum stepped back, something deep in the darkest, oldest part of his brain screamed at him to run but he shrugged it off. After all this was his son, the son they thought they had lost. He dropped the axe and reached out to hug his son. He turned his head slightly and was fascinated at the light from behind his eyes, they shone like silver discs. Callum stood still staring into those eyes, he saw his own image reflected back at him but then they seemed to open and drew him down, deeper down. He felt as though he were drowning in the deepest, sweetest water he had ever known. There was a constant singing of lullabies in his head as darkness overcame him.

Becky was horrified when their son canted his head to one side and lunged at his father. His jaw seemed to unhinge and his teeth lengthened. They slashed into Callum's throat with slick biting movements then Ally's mouth centred over the wound and he slurped greedily on the crimson blood pouring from his father's neck. It seemed to take an eternity for Becky to recover the control of her body and when she did she realised that she held the axe dropped by her dying husband. Ally let go of his father's body which slumped to the ground and he turned on his mother with vicious eyes.

"The master made me powerful Mum, he took away my disease. I can help you feel so strong and young again."

Ally lunged at her and she ducked causing him to launch himself over her.

"Get out, get out you animal," She screamed, "I don't want you to ever come back. You killed your Dad, you killed your Dad."

Ally stepped backwards towards the front door as she swung the axe in a swift arc, he stepped backwards once more and his back hit the door. She pulled back the axe and shouted once more.

"Get away, you evil bastard!"

Ally crashed backwards through the door but was a split second too slow. Becky brought the axe slicing through the air horizontally with desperate fury. The keen sharpened blade sliced through the neck of her son like the proverbial warm knife through butter cutting through the sinews, muscles, bones, arteries and veins in one fell blow. The body of her son collapsed in a heap while his head rolled backwards down the path finally settling a few yards from her facing the front gate. For a long time Becky remembered no more as unconsciousness took her. If Becky had remained conscious she would have heard the screams all over the tiny village as carnage descended upon it.

Chapter 8 Teresa

Teresa Bugatta heard the soft scraping at her bedroom window as she glanced at her LED alarm clock to check the time. A little after two am. She was still groggy from sleep and did not recognise the instinctive alarm inside her system warning her to be ready for fight or flight. She rubbed her eyes and walked to the window wondering if Boogie had forgotten his keys again. She did not remember that she had called the police along with the Maxwells to report him missing; it was too early in the morning for her memory to work that sharply. She realised it was her son before she opened the curtains, she could hear his nasally voice.

"Let me in Mum; come on let me in Mum. It's freezing out here. Let me in Mum."

She opened the curtains and was dully surprised to see her son facing her. Her room was on the first floor. *Maybe he climbed the drainpipe.* She though slowly. He stared at her and suddenly she felt she was looking at him when he was a helpless baby in her arms in the maternity hospital needing breast fed.

"Let me in Mum, come on please. Let me in, I'm freezing and I'm hungry Mum, I haven't eaten for so long. Let me in."

Teresa could not deny her little child the help he needed. All she could see was the needy little baby crying, pleading for his mother's help. She unlocked the windows and opened it.

"Come on in son, I can't have you left out in the cold." She said, her voice sleep slurred.

Boogie launched himself through the open window and grabbed his Mother and plunged his elongated canines into her neck. She sighed deeply as the bittersweet pain surged through her throat; she was letting her hungry child feed again.

Giuseppe Bugatta thought he heard a crash in his mum's room; he rubbed his eyes and looked across at the bed of his ten year old sister Teresa. She was sitting up staring at him; he could see the whites of her eyes reflecting the light from the nightlight. He was only two years older but he felt very protective of Teresa.

"Something's happened to mummy Sepp." She whispered, her eyes were wide, frightened. He thought the same as her but had to act as though he were brave so she wouldn't panic. He put one finger to his lips for her to be quiet, then he sneaked over to her bed and handed her a jumper and trousers to put on over her pyjamas

He whispered to her. "I think Daddy might have come back so we might need to hide. Put your parka and trainers on. We'll check mummy's room and if he's back we'll hide but we need to be quiet."

"Ok," she whispered and kissed his cheek. "will he leave us alone?"

"I think so. Stay behind me and if I say run then you run as fast as you can."

She nodded. Both of them were now dressed ready to leave the house if they had to.

They crept along the short upper hallway to their mother's room. Teresa stayed a step behind Sepp, her little heart was playing a tattoo in her chest. She knew her Daddy could get angry and that Mum had asked him to leave because he hurt her with a chair. She loved her Daddy but sometimes he frightened her. The last time he came back Sepp had ran away with her and they hid in the garden. Teresa knew lots of hiding places in the village but she didn't like being frightened.

Sepp slowly opened the door and was stunned by what he saw. It looked as though his older brother was kissing his mum but not in the way a boy should. He was at her neck like the way he had seen in some films.

"Alan what are you doing?" he asked, he never called his brother by his nick name.

Alan looked up from his mother's neck and focussed on his little brother and sister. Sepp took a step back and bumped into Teresa who just stood silent. Their older brother stared at them with weird silver discs for eyes, he tilted his head from side to side as he advanced on them.

"Giuseppe, Teresa, come and join us. You will be happy with us. Look Mum is happy." He gestured to their limp bodied mother, collapsed on the bed. They could see that she still breathed but she was deathly white. Teresa didn't like the way Alan looked or the sound of his voice. Alan advanced slowly, he alternated between staring at his sister then his brother.

"It only hurts a little. Like the school jag then you feel big and strong and happy. So happy. Join me. I don't want to leave you."

Sepp thought Alan looked like a vampire in the Buffy series that Teresa loved on TV, he must have been messing around with his pals and taken some drugs or something.

"Leave us alone Alan. You're acting like Dad. Look you're scaring Teresa."

Alan frowned at this for a second then suddenly spat back. "Don't talk about that animal! I'm not Dad. I won't hurt you. It is lovely - I promise."

With this he lunged at his young brother.

Sepp did not have the belief of Teresa, she realised that their brother was not just pretending to be a vampire but had in fact become one. If Sepp had realised this he might have moved quicker but he hesitated.

Alan snapped his head to the side and bit deep into Sepp's exposed neck. The young boy screamed in agony then sighed as something similar to the dentist's gas surged through him calming him down. Teresa realised this was not a film or a TV show, one of her brothers was trying to eat the other, he was a vampire. Her young mind made the quick connections and realised they had one chance and one chance only.

Alan had not yet caught up with the fact that he was a top of the food chain predator yet, he acted purely on instinct. As a first stage vampire he did not know of any weaknesses he had and ignored the little girl that had been the sister of his host. In the slow way that his vampire mind worked he just registered her as a small creature to feed on once he was finished with this second victim he had. Teresa stepped back into the hallway and took her mother's blessed crucifix holy water holder off the wall. She walked into the bedroom and shouted with a voice that seemed to have the power of an angel of vengeance.

"Get away from my brother you monster. Leave here, now!" She threw the holy water over the head of Alan and advanced with the crucifix held in front of her. The edges of the cross glowed red hot in the dimly lit room.

Alan screamed and bellowed in a cross between rage and pain as the holy water sizzled on his face. He felt tears trickle down his cheeks and let go of his brother. He didn't understand what was happening. He turned to face the door and instead of his younger sister he thought he saw a powerful creature of light behind a flaming cross. He shook his head and tried to attack but the flames forced him back and the creature roared a curse he didn't comprehend. All he knew was that he had to leave this house, his stomach lurched and his head pounded. The skin that remained unharmed on his face ached and itched. He put his arms up to protect his eyes and executed a rather inelegant back flip through the open window taking some of the frame with him.

Teresa looked around the room stunned that she had managed to scare off the vampire that now controlled her oldest brother. She held grimly to the cross and looked at her brother Sepp who winced at the sight of the holy item, her Mother did the same but she was more alert. She put her hand up to protect her eyes from the bright flames and spoke in a crackled voice.

"Teresa, you must run away and hide somewhere my little angel. I didn't know he was a vampire. I think I'm going to turn into one and Sepp will too. You need to go somewhere we can't find you and hide until help comes. I can't protect you now my darling. Run and hide before he comes back. I love you baby.

Tears rolled down Teresa's cheeks, she rubbed them with the sleeve of her parka and looked at the remains of her family for one last time.

"I love you too Mummy, and you Sepp, and you Alan." She whispered and ran out of the room and down the stairs. She reached up to unlock the front door and looked from left to right before running out into the snow. Screams could be heard from neighbouring houses. She sobbed softly but a special calmness stayed within her as she clutched her mum's crucifix close to her. She knew where she could hide until morning. As safe a place as she could think of and neither her mum nor Sepp knew about it.

Chapter 9 Seige Over

It was a couple of minutes before any of them could speak. Steven had switched on a television screen in the mess room where they could see the cctv footage from the different cameras. The men from the gate seemed to have left. Steven had poured tea for all of them and they sat drinking in silence.

Tom looked over at Claire. "What happened? You were meant to warn me if anything was wrong."

"You arrived just as I stepped out, Tom," she explained. "I was looking at the cctv cameras and it seemed that a deer launched itself over the fence and its head ripped off. I know how crazy that sounds and I now know that isn't what happened but that was how it looked at the time. The alarms went off and I opened the door I could hear you both running and so I decided to check the deer. I had reached it when those three creeps arrived and then you joined me and you know the rest."

Claire looked across at Steven

"Was that your colleagues?"

Steven nodded sadly "Or what is left of them. "They really creeped me out. Did either of you see their eyes?"

"Like crocodile's eyes." Claire said.

"I thought of sharks." Tom said. "I think we felt the same thing though. I felt as if they were sizing me up as dinner. This is just ridiculous. Things like that can not exist. They must be on drugs or something. That might explain they way they talked."

"The hissing was dreadful. Almost like the way you would imagine a snake talking." Claire put in.

Tom didn't like all these analogies with predatory animals but somehow it felt correct. The three men had seemed like predators and he had for the first time in his life felt like a hunted animal must.

"Why didn't they rush us when we were out near the jeep and why didn't they damage the jeep to stop us leaving?" he asked to no one in particular.

Steven shrugged and hunched further over the table.

Claire stared into space for a moment." It really has to be the running water. I think Steven taking back the invitation helped as well. I don't know if the deer landing near the jeep was meant to damage it or if it was just to set off the alarms so that we would come out into the open. Part of me thinks they don't care if we leave in the jeep. They don't seem to consider us a threat. I wonder if it is in the same way that a shark thinks nothing of the seals it hunts or a cat after a mouse even."

Tom thought about that for a second. He did not know which disturbed him more the jeep being rendered useless or the fact that someone or something could be so dismissive of two police officers and a third man who wasn't exactly helpless. He did not like this, he did not like it at all. He leant forward on the table and looked at the TV screen, the men were still gone. Tom checked his watch it was just after 4 am.

"Claire why didn't you wake me?"

She flushed slightly then answered.

"I could sleep on the way back but you needed to be fresh. I was going to wake you around now but I guess you won't sleep anymore?"

Tom shook his head. "Not a chance in hell."

It seemed to take forever but eventually the sun rose. The three of them had taken turns at watching the cctv screen so they knew that no harm had come to the jeep. They quickly gathered their gear and prepared to leave. Steven looked around for a second making sure he hadn't forgotten anything then asked.

"Do you not need heavy coats? I have some spare parkas here."

Tom shook his head. "We have heavy coats in the back of the jeep if we need them. We should be ok though."

Claire tightened her equipment belt around her while Tom did the same. They stared at one another for a few seconds.

"It looks like they haven't returned. I want to check around the jeep but you both climb inside while I do and then we will leave."

The three of them opened the door to the outside and were immediately hit with two things. It was freezing cold and it was amazingly bright. The clouds that had brought all the snow had dispersed leaving a clear blue sky while the sun reflected brilliantly of the white expanse of snow.

Tom pressed the unlock button on his key and Steven and Claire ran across and climbed into the jeep. Tom checked around the perimeter of the jeep but there were no footprints in the pristine snow and he decided to try the ignition. He climbed inside and put the keys in the ignition. The jeep jumped into life instantly. Tom let out a quiet prayer of thanks and glanced round the jeep. Claire gave a little cheer and Steven patted him on the shoulder. Tom gradually accelerated out of the compound and turned left to head towards Cothqon the jeep slewed slightly as they climbed the hill into the woods.

Cothqon was smaller than a village, barely a hamlet nestled in a high pass near the top of the mountain. If the housing had still been mainly the cottages that had originally made up the settlement rather than their 1970's replacements it could have been picturesque. Instead it looked dismal and depressing. It reminded Claire of so many small villages she had visited as a teenager when going to see friends around the area.

"Do you know Cothqon Claire?" Tom asked while squinting out the window as they approached what seemed to be the main road through the village. Claire looked around at the houses and answered.

"Yeah sort of. I had a friend who stayed here when I was at high school and it doesn't look as though it has changed. There is this road and there is one that runs parallel to the left of us. There are only about fifteen or twenty houses. There is a farmhouse on the main road as you go down the other side of the mountain and that's it I think. God the place looks dead."

"Unfortunate choice of words." Added Steven from the back. He hadn't realised how scared he was until now, he just wanted to get to a major town. He looked out the windows either side of him.

"I think the best way of seeing if there is anyone here is to put on the siren and lights and see if we get a reaction." Claire suggested.

"Yeah," Tom agreed, "I will do it for a few seconds at a time then switch off to see if we hear anyone."

Tom switched on the lights and the siren and intermittently switched them off as they drove along the main road and then turned down a connecting street to the back road without seeing a reaction. They were halfway along the back road when they saw something that caused them to draw to a halt. A mid-terraced house had a half kicked in door and a human head lay in the garden.

"Oh, shit!" Tom muttered. He looked at Claire and wondered whether they should investigate.

Chapter 10 Rescue Arrives

Becky Maxwell hunkered close to the curtained upstairs window of her council house. She thought that she had heard a police siren but did not want to get her hopes up. Things seemed to be better in the daylight but she did not know how to drive so wasn't confident of getting down the mountain before darkness but if the police arrived she could be saved. Part of her wondered if it was some sort of trick though. The strange creatures that their children had become had already shown they were capable of carrying out any number of ruses to gain access to homes and killing the occupants. As far as Becky was aware she was the lone survivor. She watched as the police jeep stopped outside her gate. They must have noticed the head of her son in the front garden. She decided to take the chance but took her axe with her anyway.

Tom had climbed out of the jeep and Claire was just opening her door when a bedraggled figure emerged from the house carrying an axe. Tom's hand went towards his truncheon and the female figure slowed down and let the axe drop to her side. Tom realised that the woman was upset but not ready to attack. She actually looked relieved.

"Thank God," She exclaimed, " I thought they had come up with another trick to try and get me. Please get us out of here."

She dropped the axe and put her arms around Tom sobbing. Tom put an arm around her and helped her to the jeep. Steven opened the door and helped her inside. Tom climbed back in as did Claire and they drove away.

Claire turned round to face the woman and began to speak. "Who are you Madame? We have been searching for anyone in the village we had reports of people being missing.".

"My name is Becky Maxwell. As far as I know I'm the only person alive from Cothqon. The way those animals were going last night I can't imagine anyone else surviving. My God my own son tried to rip me apart." Her hands came up to cover her face as she relived the horror of it all again. "My son was one of the boys reported missing. They all returned the night before last and we were happy to see them. The minute we let Ally in he attacked my husband, his Dad. I had to…I had to fight him off. I forced him out and shouted that he would never be allowed back home. He attacked me and…well you saw the end result on the lawn. I have been hiding ever since. Can you take me to the police station please? I will tell you everything there - I just want out of here."

"Don't worry Mrs Maxwell," Clare said, putting her arm around her. "We're heading there just now. There are some parkas on the parcel shelf behind you. Put one on to keep yourself warm."

Tom accelerated along the road and it wasn't long before they passed the outlying farmhouse Claire had mentioned. He heard the whirring noise of a helicopter somewhere nearby. Claire wound down the passenger window and stuck her head out. She ducked back in and reported.

"There is an army chopper up above us." Tom didn't answer but stared ahead and hit the brakes causing the jeep to slow rapidly. Claire scowled for a second then looked forward. A pair of armoured vehicles blocked the road and armed soldiers stood facing them. A sergeant signalled for them to stop as the soldiers approached nervously moving their guns. Tom wound down the window and the tall sergeant ducked to speak to him.

"Good morning officers, Sir, Madame. This area is subject to a state of emergency and under military control. I am going to have to ask you all to come with me to one of our trucks where you will be taken to a debriefing area. Nothing to worry about you will just be checked over by medics and our C.O. will want to chat with you then you should be able to go on your way. One of my men will follow you in this jeep so that you can drive back to the police station."

Tom knew not to argue too much, even though the sergeant was being polite he knew the men would have strict orders to ensure that anyone who was stopped obeyed them. He had to try and find out what was happening though.

"No problem Sergeant," He said, "Do you have any idea what has happened? We were ordered to check out the village at the summit as many of the people were missing and to bring anyone we met down with us."

The Sergeant shook his head slowly. " I was just told to expect a police jeep and ask the occupants to go in our truck. I was told the same as you about the village but we only arrived at first light. If you want to know anymore you will need to ask the boss. You know how it is for us Sergeants." He offered a friendly smile.

Tom reckoned the sergeant knew more than he was letting on but decided not to push it. He noticed that apart from rank badges none of the soldiers had any other adornment to signify their units or names. That was unusual. The army sergeant opened Tom's door while other soldiers did the same with the other three. As Tom got out a lanky corporal stepped into the driving seat of the police jeep.

"Don't worry I'll drive her as if she were my own Sergeant." He quipped.

Tom nodded at him.

The four of them walked through the roadblock escorted by two troopers and the sergeant. Tom noticed the armoured vehicles had .50 cal machine guns manned by grim faced men pointed back up the road they had come along. He glanced up and saw what he recognised as a Blackhawk helicopter hovering above them. They got to the truck and a soldier in the rear helped each of them up into the truck while the two escorts climbed in behind them. The sergeant fastened the rear gate. He shouted above the growl of the diesel engine.

"Don't worry you are safe now. Her Majesty's finest are covering your back."

He smacked the back of the truck with his gun butt and the truck pulled away. He offered a formal salute to Tom who couldn't help but smile at meeting a kindred spirit. The sergeant turned back to the roadblock, he was nervous about this latest job, very nervous. He tapped the wooden bayonet in the scabbard on his belt and hoped the special bullets they had in their guns and the other weapons would work. If not, he did not know what they would do but he supposed that was what the Boss got paid the big bucks to worry about.

Chapter 11 The Camp

Tom was the first of the group to get out of the truck when they stopped at what was obviously a hastily erected camp. He noticed that the camp seemed to be surrounded by streams and water filled ditches. He nodded towards one of these and Claire gave the briefest of nods in return. The corporal who had driven their jeep behind the truck now led them towards a tent that had several aerials protruding from it. When they entered the tent they were greeted by a young looking Major with a short beard.

"Good morning ladies and gentlemen. I am afraid for the time being we will need to split you up for a little while. The Colonel would like to speak to both Police officers while our medics check over both Steven and Rebecca?" All four of the group were surprised that this Major knew their names already. The Major beckoned for Steven and Rebecca to follow the Corporal towards a tent clearly marked with a red cross while he led the police officers further into the tent.

"Excuse me Major but why are we being separated?" Tom asked.

"Nothing to worry about Sergeant. We are looking for all four of you to assist us. The other two have not signed the official secrets act yet but they will after they have been given a check up and been given a shower and fresh clothes. You on the other hand have signed the act and being public servants like myself you will no doubt be keen to exchange information with the Boss."

He marched briskly and they followed him past two guards and entered a room where a Colonel sat on a deck chair talking on a satellite phone.

The colonel beckoned for them to sit on seats facing him and smiled warmly as he finished his call. "Yes of course Mr Secretary Sir. I will keep you informed if this goes beyond my delegated powers. Thank you sir and good morning to you too."

A large map table sat between the new arrivals and the Colonel, it was covered with maps of the local area with various areas circled and pencil marks here there and everywhere. In front of the Colonel was a laptop and he closed the cover of this as they sat down. As the Colonel leaned forward resting his elbows on the table Tom noticed that he also had no insignia on his tunic which he wore unzipped halfway down with an undershirt visible beneath it.

"Ah Tom, Claire, I am Colonel Tim Forbes. Forgive the theatrics but we only received confirmation that you were within the quarantine zone about thirty minutes ago and we were still setting up checkpoints. I hope you were not too alarmed?"

"We didn't expect to see armed soldiers." Claire blurted out. The Colonel held his hands up.

"As I said please forgive the theatrics. We needed to be sure it was you that was coming out and not some of these," He paused as if searching for the correct word. "killers."

Tom sat back in his chair and folded his arms.

"The Major here said you would like to exchange information. Could you please tell us Colonel why the army have sealed off a sizeable area of southern Scotland?"

"Of course Sergeant." He looked at both of them, steepled his fingers and began. "As you will be aware from your experiences overnight something strange has happened to this area recently. People have disappeared and there seems to have been brutal murders in the area. We believe this is down to a contagion of sorts and it may be linked to similar incidents in the past that the army needed to contain. Hence our presence, we are a specialist army unit specifically trained and equipped for dealing with these sort of incidents. I have been given specific orders to first of all contain this outbreak and then once this has been achieved to find the source and eradicate it."

"I will try and answer any questions you have afterwards within the parameters of your need to know but now I would like to ask you some questions."

Both Tom and Claire nodded, it was only then that they noticed the soldier sitting with a laptop who began typing a note.

Forbes scratched his shaven head for a second while carefully watching both of the Police.

"I have a series of questions about what you saw to help me confirm if this is what I think it is. First of all, did you see any bodies or evidence of murders?"

"Yes, we saw copious amounts of matted blood and what seemed to be chunks of flesh in the student's tents at the archaeological dig down by the loch." Tom answered.

"The only actual body we saw was in Cothqon, we saw a torso and severed head in a garden there but Becky claims that was her son and she killed him." Claire added. The typist clicked away on the laptop. Forbes expression did not change.

"Did you see any of the, for want of a better word, killers?"

"We didn't actually see them kill anyone but we saw three of them, yes." Claire replied.

Forbes formed a pyramid with his hands, he looked from Claire to Tom and back to Claire again.

"Could you give me a description of them please? As much detail as you can."

"They seemed human," Claire began, "but there was something strange with their eyes. They were sort of silver and seemed lit from behind in the same way that a cat's or dog's eyes look when your car headlights catch them except there wasn't much light shining on them. They also seemed to speak with a lisp and the voices were so inhuman and cold." She looked at Tom for confirmation and he nodded then he continued for her.

"There is something else that I remember noticing at the time. They were standing in snow that was at least two inches deep and yet never left any footprints."

"Jesus,!" Claire interrupted, " now that you mention it, there were no footprints. How can fully grown men cross snow covered roads and not leave footprints?"

"Do you want to tell the Colonel your theories Claire?" Tom asked raising an eyebrow. Claire flushed slightly but she wasn't going to give Tom that satisfaction of putting her off.

The colonel raised his eyebrows.

She coughed slightly to pluck up the courage and began. "I did a lot of research on the so called accidents, disappearances and murders in this area over the last thirty years and beyond for my university dissertation. As crazy as it sounds I came to the one and only conclusion you can from all of this. There are creatures in these hills that seem to be vampires. As far as I am concerned if it looks like a vampire and acts like a vampire then it is a vampire." She looked at Forbes for a reaction but his expression gave nothing away.

"Do you have more to add Claire?" He asked.

"Yes, there seems to be two different ways the people are killed. Either a body is found with the head removed and clots of flesh all around the area or no body is found. In the second case relatives report being disturbed by visits of the missing relative over the next few nights. The relatives then vanish or leave the area."

Claire sat back in her chair and waited to be ridiculed. Instead Forbes clapped his hands and smiled at her. "Bravo, Claire, Bravo. I think we may need to offer you a post with us, no offence but your talents are wasted in the police."

She tried to pick up if he was mocking her but he seemed to be genuine. He leant forward. "We have gathered similar intelligence to what you have discovered. It seems that for whatever reason whether it be a freak of nature or supernature if you like that there are indeed vampire like creatures here. I will give you a brief resume of what the army is aware of within what I am allowed to discuss. In the darkest moments of world war two our country faced invasion from what I personally believe to be the most evil regime the world has ever produced. One of my predecessors was instructed by the government of the day to devise supernatural weapons that we could use in the event of an invasion. This officer was a keen history scholar and knew of the legends about vampires being entombed in the church at Deil on the shores of the Black Loch. A specialist army unit was ordered to find the tombs and discover if they could raise these vampires and use them to defend the area."

"From what I understand the officer was successful in raising these vampires but could not control them. They had a disaster on their hands, fortunately the village had been evacuated but a sizeable number of the troops were killed before the officer could once more entomb the vampires. The only thing is that as you pointed out Claire there seem to have been deaths and disappearances in the intervening years that would suggest that somehow the vampires could still get out but were perhaps constrained to a specific area."

"Perhaps not all of them were entombed?" Claire suggested.

Forbes nodded slowly.

"That is a possibility. There seem to be three types of these creatures. The most powerful are what we term type ones. This is the creatures that were in the tombs they are either born vampires or are very old converts and can move exceedingly quickly and seem to have powerful hypnotic ability along with other abilities that we are not aware of yet. They do not seem to need to feed very often and can hibernate for long periods. The second type of type twos are converts, that is they have been bitten and turned in the way that you see in movies. They are slower than the type ones and only seem to be slightly stronger and perhaps faster than humans but are vicious and need a lot of feeding. They are I suppose like type one children."

"The final versions are the type threes. These would seem to be the ones that cause the meat shredding effect on victims. These are the slowest of the three and never seem to develop the way that the type twos will. They act quite like zombies from movies but move quicker and are strong. They seem to need the most blood and eat some of the flesh too. We don't really know why some of the converts become type threes rather than two. It might be part of their genetic make up, it might be because their attacker takes too long feeding on them. Who knows? All we know is that they rip the heads off of their victims so unlike the other two types they don't reproduce their numbers. These are the easiest ones to catch and kill."

Claire's brows shot up. "So you know how to kill these creatures? Are the legends true? Stakes through the heart, sunlight etc?"

Forbes nodded slowly.

"Some of the legends are true. Yes it would seem from past records that you can kill them with either a stake through the heart or by exposing them to sunlight. Decapitation seems to be effective too. The stake through the heart seems to work through lodging itself in the heart and experiments were carried out with bullets that contained ash, hawthorn or iron that flatten themselves inside the heart killing the creatures. We have our men armed with specially modified bullets that should work in this manner. We also have holy water with us and blessed Eucharistic wafers. It all sounds like classic horror film mumbo jumbo but my predecessors all reported that these worked along with burning the bodies. Fire as a purifier was how my second world war colleague termed it." A trace of a smile crept along his lips.

Tom scratched the stubble on his cheeks. "I can't believe that I am asking a question like this but we discussed the possibility of running water acting as a barrier to these creatures. From what we saw at the compound they at least don't seem fond of crossing it."

"It would seem so," Forbes agreed, "You may have noticed that this camp is surrounded by streams? We diverted the stream into two to ensure we had this as a form of protective moat. The vampires, let's call them that, seem to have been entombed under the church with a running stream keeping them on one side of a chamber. Again I got this from the Second World War records. I can only presume that the archaeological dig must have diverted the water somehow and released them by accident. Our problem now is how we hunt down these creatures and kill or capture them. I know from experience we can kill the type two and three but I am not certain we can kill the type one vampires." He opened his hands leaving them palms up on the table.

"There you have it. I have told you all that I can think of to help you. If you have any questions as we go on I will do my best to answer but for now I ask that you give me your full cooperation to sort this situation out. What do you say?"

Tom and Claire looked at one another for a second then answered in unison.

"Yes."

Forbes smiled and opened his arms. "In that case welcome to my little camp. We will organise beds for you both and you will have access to the mess and showers. Once you are rested I will talk to you some more and you can help me to contain and eradicate this problem. With God's help we shall succeed."

It was only when Forbes said this that Tom noticed he had a crucifix round his neck. The Major appeared behind them and gave a little coughed to announce his presence. "I will show you both to your lodgings." He joked.

They followed the Major through a labyrinth of tents until he eventually stopped at a medium sized tent that was obviously recently erected. Two camp beds sat within it with bedding neatly folded on top of them. The Major gestured around the interior.

"This will be your accommodation until you rest and then hopefully we can let you get home tomorrow. There is a small heater over there if you get cold but there are fresh army clothes in those boxes for you that should keep you warm and help you feel a bit more human. I am afraid they might not fit exactly but at least they are clean. There are showers just through that way, the ladies in our unit have a separate shower. We are not complete barbarians. Well I will let you make yourselves at home."

With that the Major left them alone. Tom closed over the tent entrance and turned to Claire.

"Something isn't right here, Claire."

"You feel it too?" She asked keeping her voice hushed. He nodded.

"They obviously can't tell us everything but I think they won't let us leave tomorrow." He paused, thought for a second and added.

"Did you notice that Forbes said they found out the bullets worked in experiments?"

Claire jumped at this.

"That means they must have had vampires to test on or their victims."

"Yes, which might explain the deaths over the years, perhaps one of these escaped."

Tom thought about it all for a moment.

"The more I think of this Claire the less I like it. I think we are in the middle of an experiment that has gone wrong which would explain the large army presence."

"What do we do then Tom? It's not likely that they will let us just walk away."

"Assuming they manage a proper mopping up operation they can. We won't have any evidence of what happened here. To be perfectly honest as long as I get away from here I don't care how they clear this up. I just want to get home and have a long hot shower. Talking of which…" He nodded towards the showers.

Claire smiled and raised her eyebrows. "Don't you be trying to get an eyeful of me in my shower." They walked over to the boxes and picked up the army uniforms and were glad to see some fresh towels in the boxes and army issue underwear. Claire lifted up a pair of khaki briefs and laughed holding them against her waist. They took the clothes and towels then headed towards the showers.

Chapter 12 A Conversation

Colonel Forbes read through some of the files on his armoured lap top, he looked up as Major Blood ambled into the main area of the tent. A slight smile ghosted his face, Blood still had the swagger of a paratrooper.

"Joseph, are our guests settling in?"

"Yes, Tim, and as you suspected they realised what the situation is."

Forbes stretched and clasped his hands behind his head, he nodded to one of the chairs and Blood sat down.

"This is for the best. They will help us in the end if we need them but the more they think we are keeping them in the dark the less they will interfere."

"I'm not so sure Tim. The Sergeant is former forces and the girl is no mug. I can understand this approach with the civvies, they are close to hysteria but both Tom and Claire have made astute observations. Plus, the four of them are the only people to have survived a night among these things."

Forbes looked at his second in command and old friend contemplating. "Not many of us have done that Joseph."

"Not many." Blood agreed. Forbes fingered his crucifix while he thought this over. He leant back again stretching once more.

"Now and again I remember why I brought you across from the parachute regiment with me."

"Ah but in those days you were green slime Tim. Still can't believe you passed parachute school to get attached to us." Blood smiled.

"Sometimes the ends justify the means. I think you are correct about the police. I will fill them in and seek their cooperation. We will inform the civilians as well but they will need to be protected."

Chapter 13 Teresa and the Priest

Teresa ate the bread carefully that the old priest had given her. He had gathered together some food and cans of coke into a small knapsack and placed this over his shoulder. Teresa glanced up at the hole in the crypt door and saw the shaft of daylight poking through and felt safer at once. She had been through a terrible night hearing the screams of the others in the village throughout the hours of darkness. As far as they were aware they were the only two people alive in the village.

"Do you think we will be safe in daylight father? In Buffy it is safe."

"I am sure we will be safe Teresa we will just need to be quiet as mice while we walk down the hill. We might get lucky and find a car."

Teresa thought it would be great if they found a car but she was sure the vampires would not have made things so easy for them. She has seen enough horror shows and films to know they were really smart. She felt comforted by the rosary beads that hung round her neck, the heavy cross was a security blanket of sorts giving her strength. She looked at the priest for a sign that they should move.

Father O'Reilly climbed up the steps of the crypt and carefully unlocked the doors before flinging them open. Bright daylight surged in dazzling them with the brilliance of it as sunlight reflected off the fresh snow. O'Reilly looked around the small church yard satisfied that no one was waiting in ambush nearby.

"Let's go Teresa. Now remember if anything happens to me just run down the road. Don't wait on me, you must get away."

Teresa nodded slowly, she understood at a deep level that she was meant to make it out of the village.

"We are going to see some horrible things on our way out of here so try not to look too carefully okay?"

Teresa nodded again. She did not want to see the things that would be here but she had to walk down the main road at least she had a priest with her. As they walked along she could see red and black streaks at various intervals in the white backdrop of snow that covered the village. She took Father O'Reilly's advice and did not look too closely. Some of the streaks had piles of flesh at the end of them and these reminded her of when their cat had brought back half dead birds as presents. That always grossed her out; she did not want to think too much about what these presents were. She glanced up at the priest and saw that his face was pallid and there were tears glistening in his eyes. She tucked her hands into the pockets of her parka and drew her chin into the collar against the snow. *Think happy thoughts* she told herself and concentrated on getting off the hillside.

Chapter 14 More Survivors

Tom and Claire felt bemused as they were led back to the command tent by Major Blood. There seemed to be a furore in the camp and Blood had refused to fill them in. Tom noticed a truck being unloaded at the back of the camp as they passed. A large number of dogs were jumping around and barking as they were led from the truck towards what looked lie makeshift kennels. As they reached the tent, he pulled back the flap and gestured for them to go in and he followed them. A couple of rifleman stood behind the Colonel at ease with their carbines slung across their chests. Seated across from Forbes were an elderly cleric and a girl who looked as though she were still of primary school age. Forbes smiled towards the police officers and gestured for them to sit down. He then spoke to the riflemen who snapped to attention and left the tent to guard its entrance.

"Good news officers, good news. We have found two more survivors. Father Damien O'Reilly and Teresa Bugatta I would like to introduce Sergeant Tom McKillop and Constable Claire Lawell."

Claire gave a warm smile to the little girl and exchanged pleasantries while Tom and the priest shook hands. Claire nodded a friendly greeting as they sat down. Forbes laid his hands on the table face up and sighed with obvious effort.

"I have spoken things over with my able second in command," He gestured to Blood then went on, "We had already agreed to bring you properly up to speed so that we can work together. I will do that in a moment but we have since found out more information from this charming ten year old heroine." He nodded towards Teresa who blushed slightly and smiled.

"It turns out that Teresa knew how to chase off the vampires and her story is similar to my introduction to this field. I think it will help us to clear the area of them."

Tom stretched to get the tension out of his body, then he said,. "We assumed that you weren't giving us the full story Colonel so it isn't a big surprise. We will do our best to help."

"Okay," Forbes said, "the unit that I command here deals with situations like this more often than you would imagine. It is not the first time that I personally have had to deal with these creatures. As you may have guessed by the faint traces in my accent I hail from these parts and many years ago I was involved in a car crash over on the next hill. There were four of us in the car and three of us survived the crash but I was the only one to make it off the hill. We were ambushed by what we thought was a young women. She moved with incredible speed and killed two of my friends. I was terrified but somewhere deep inside me a comforting voice told me to use the cross round my neck and command her to back off in God's name. I had always been religious but up until then it had just been a case of going to mass on a Sunday and the odd confession. On that winter's night though I had my road to Damascus moment. I saw that there was pure evil in the world and I also learnt that there is an elemental good force in the world that could be channelled to save us." He paused. "Forgive me if I sound like an evangelist but it had a profound effect on me. Somehow I was guided to chase off the vampire. She fled into the night and I swear that the cross glowed in my hands. The voice instructed me to walk down the mountain road and that I would be safe. It was after that I went to a seminary and from there became an army chaplain and long story short I ended up in command of the occult bureau. Anyway I will let Teresa explain what happened to her before I bring you up to speed on what we aim to do and what we require of you."

Forbes nodded and smiled gently to Teresa who had Father O'Reilly's arm on her shoulders. She held a cup of water and took a sip then spoke with a quiet but confident voice.

"My big brother and me heard noises in Mummy's room last night. We thought our Daddy was back. He gets drunk and is mean to Mummy, he shouts lots and I think he punches her." She paused for a sip of water and looked at the people in the room then went on.

"Sepp and I went into her room and we saw Alan there."

"Her older brother." Forbes silently mouthed to the police officers.

"He was biting Mummy's neck. Like the way vampires on Buffy do it." She tilted her head to the side and mimed a vampire bite.

"I tried to tell Sepp. He got too near and Alan bit him too. I think God or an Angel told me what to do. I got Mummy's holy water and cross and told the monster to get out. Alan did a weird somersault thing and jumped out. My cross lit up too like Mr Forbes' did. Mummy told me to hide. I ran out and hid in the chapel. I climbed in the back door to the crypt and met Father O'Reilly. God and the Angels kept us safe and then we came here." She sniffed and rubbed tears from her eyes. "I miss my Mummy and Alan and Sepp. They're dead now. The vampires just look like them …but they aren't them." Teresa gave a quiet sob and she snuggled against the old priest.

Father O'Reilly softly patted the little girl's back he looked over at the Police officers and spoke, his accent a strange mixture of Scottish and Northern Irish. "Teresa or God through her saved my life last night. She came in the back way to the chapel through the crypt and surprised me just as I was about to go out the front door to help someone who was hurt. Turns out it was a vampire's trick. They couldn't come into the chapel and were trying to lure me out. She did the same thing with the cross that you already heard and the creature backed away hissing like a wounded cat. It was only then I recognised her as my housekeeper. As strange as all this sounds it wasn't the strangest thing to happen. Teresa seemed to have a booming voice as she instructed me to lock the doors with cords and she spoke in Latin over them. I swear that light flowed down her arms and over the cords, the doors seemed to have lightning crawling over them for a moment then it all went dark. If I hadn't been tee total for thirty years I would have thought I was hallucinating. I felt very safe last night, it seemed that we were being guarded by one of God's angels."

Teresa visibly blushed at this but sat up, her eyes were dry now and said softly. "I wish I was an Angel. I would go after the vampires and send them to hell."

Claire marvelled at how children dealt with things. She was convinced that if had witnessed her brother turn into a vampire and kill the rest of her family she would be catatonic.

Tom shook his head slowly and leant forward his face in his hands. "I feel as if I am in the twilight zone. If I hadn't seen these things for myself……." He left the thought hanging. Forbes nodded at him, he leant back once more in his chair and continued.

"As you can all see there are similarities in our experiences with these … these creatures. They are not the soft doey eyed romantic creatures that recent films have shown. These are living or rather living dead monsters that feed on humans. We are just sources of sustenance for them. Nothing more, nothing less. If we do not hunt them down while there are only a small number of them then it will be two late. To misquote the hero in Salem's Lot; one makes two, two make four, four make eight and before you know it whole towns are gone."

"I have hunted these creatures in the past and normally they have been wary, only attacking now and again. We have usually killed them in a short space of time but this time it is different. The legends of this area are true as we discussed. We think that one of the creatures managed to escape the second world war cordon and survived in the hills. I don't know if we killed the original one over the years that we hunted it or if we just continually killed its offspring so to speak. It does seem however that it was preparing the way for when its master would be released."

"You saw our men at a roadblock when you came down the hill but what you did not see is the sensors we have set up around the hill. These form an invisible cordon that the vampires can't cross without us knowing about it. At the moment we have the situation contained but very soon we will want to eradicate the threat. I have requested reinforcements and by tomorrow morning I will have enough troops to search the hill with a fine tooth comb. The whole thing should be cleaned up by the end of the week. I have a thorough plan to ensure that we do not leave any unit isolated and vulnerable. What we need though is as much information as all of you and our two other guests can give about where you saw the creatures and estimates of numbers. From this we can work out as best as possible how many of these things we are facing and where they may be hiding. I am sorry to ask you to go through this but we will need you to come in with us when we attack."

Forbes raised his eyebrows in question and waited,

"Yes," Teresa said, a determined frown on her face.

Father O'Reilly sat silently fingering his rosary beads.

Tom and Claire looked at one another, and then they both nodded.

"Excellent," said Forbes, "my officers will talk with you individually to work out what everyone knows. Following that my plans will be amended, I will then work out who goes with which units as we go in. You will have plenty of protection though, believe me I do not want to lose anyone else to these vile creatures."

It was some time later that Tom and Claire managed to get some time together in their accommodation tent to compare notes. To their complete non surprise they had been asked virtually the same questions so the army unit were obviously working to a set routine. This gave Tom a bit of comfort as it seemed the army did know what they were doing.

"Penny for your thoughts Tom." Claire murmured.

Tom sat on his camp bed staring at a map of the area spread out before him.

"I am just trying to work out what the soldiers will do next. My guess is that there must be checkpoints out near the post office and that they will aim to man the Scottish power compound seeing as it seems to be secure from attack. They will then be able to send out attacks from here, the post office side and there."

Claire came over and sat on the edge of the bed to look at the map. She pointed towards the site of the archaeology dig.

"They will be able to seal off the dig area by road but that won't stop the vampires going cross country. They will need lots of soldiers to seal the whole area."

Tom stroked his chin looking at the map, she was correct it was a huge area.

"Colonel Forbes mentioned them using sensors to form a cordon. They could have set them out by jeep or motor bike. The helicopters would allow them to race troops to any point where the cordon was breached. I think that's how they must be doing it."

"You missed one thing." Claire pointed out. She thumbed over her shoulder. "The dogs we saw getting brought in. All the legends say vampires hate and fear dogs. I am not sure why it might be something to do with dogs seeing through their disguise and warning people. Whatever the reason, Colonel Forbes has brought in a whole load of them and I bet my mortgage that there are more on the other side of the hill."

Chapter 15 A Plan is Hatched

Some time later Forbes reconvened a meeting with all of the survivors and Major Blood in his command tent. Darkness had fallen and the soldiers guarding the tent understandably seemed more on edge. They all sat in a semi circle around Forbes' desk with him as the central point while he held court.

"As far as we are aware the six of you are the only survivors from the vampire attacks in the last week. You are as safe as you can be here in the middle of our camp. Some of you understand the lore of vampires so I don't need to tell you that we need to hunt down the vampires for you to be safe. From my experience once they have your scent they seem to hunt you until either you or they are dead. Therefore your best chance is to help us to hunt them down and eradicate the threat."

He pointed to a white board over his shoulder. "With this in mind I have divided you into two groups so that we can use your knowledge to best effect. Becky, Damian and Teresa will be in the group that searches Cothqon tomorrow morning I assume that between you we should have knowledge of most of the places that the creatures could hide up. Following that the group you are in will set fire to the village and head on to join up with the group led by Major Blood. This group will include Tom, Claire and Steven and as you will probably have guessed you will be tasked with checking out the Scottish Power compound." He looked over at the manager. "Steven, you will have more knowledge on the site. My aim is for Joseph to set up a strongpoint in the compound so that we can divide the hill into sectors and then carry out search and destroy missions until we can clear the area. Joseph will radio back to here to inform us when his group have arrived and then once more when both groups met up. From what you have told my men it would seem that the compound will be a safe area for you to be billeted until we succeed in this mission. If it isn't then two sections of my men should have enough firepower to fight your way through to here."

"I want you all to have a good nights sleep, we will be leaving at first light. Your section leaders will come and collect you for the missions in the morning. I cannot emphasise enough how much we appreciate your help and want to assure you that everything that can be done will be done to keep you safe. I will probably not see you in the morning so I want to wish you all good luck and ask that God looks over us all."

Forbes held out his hands in the form of a priest offering a blessing to his clergy. Tom was astonished that he did not feel self conscious bowing his head to accept the blessing, he looked out of the side of his eye and saw all of his companions doing the same. They all stood up and walked off to their respective tents, each silently brooding over what the day ahead of them would bring.

Chapter 16 a Sudden Attack

Claire woke with a start, falling out of the camp bed. There was a horrendous din as a claxon blared, and the sound of soldiers' voices trying to call above it. She lay for a few moments, her mind a dull muddle as she tried to work out what was going on. It felt as though she had just fallen asleep but she could see that it was fully dark outside their tent. Tom was already up and about zipping up his heavy DPM Gore-Tex jacket. Then she heard the sound of rapid gun fire.

"What is going on?" She screamed at Tom,

"We are under attack Claire!" he shouted back. "The soldiers are firing at vampires. One of the sentries told me as he ran by to give back up to those on the perimeter."

Claire then realised what Tom had picked up: a snub nosed machine gun. "Where did you get that?" She demanded.

Tom pulled back the charging lever and checked that a round was chambered before putting the safety catch on. "One of the sentries gave me it. They asked did I know how to use it as they need every person they can get to defend the perimeter. Do you know how to use a gun?"

"I fired a shotgun a few times but I think those things are a bit more complex." She smiled weakly.

"Okay I will show you later but come with me and stay close."

Claire nodded, rubbed her eyes then slipped on her boots. When she was ready, Tom led her back towards the entrance to the camp where most of the shots were coming from.

The rat-a-tat of controlled machine gun fire could be heard above the klaxon alarm while section leaders shouted out instructions. Suddenly above it all a fast boom boom boom could be heard.

"What the hell is that?" Claire exclaimed shouting above the cacophony.

"The 50 cal guns must be opening up. Impressive aren't they?" Tom grinned.

"You're actually enjoying this aren't you?" She scolded.

He shook his head. "No, it's just the rush of battle. Had it before. Stay close, this might get very scary very quickly."

He ran towards the noise, Claire followed muttering to herself. "Like it isn't scary already."

She followed Tom as he weaved this way and that through neat rows of tents and columns of ammunition and equipment boxes. She saw Tom tap the ammunition pouches on the webbing belt he had put on in the tent. She felt very exposed with only a truncheon to defend herself. This was lunacy.

They finally reached the perimeter of the camp where a few dozen camouflage clad soldiers were set out in a skirmish line between warrior armoured vehicles. The men were in various poses firing their weapons into the forest. The warrior vehicles shone powerful searchlights that created avenues of daylight within the blackness of the trees. Tom ran up to an officer who was reloading his carbine, took a look at his rank patch and said.

"Captain, I was told you need all the weapons men you can get. Where do you need me?"

The young officer looked confused for a second then visibly composed himself. "Join the right hand side of my skirmish line sergeant but do not cross the trench. Shoot anything that comes at you." Tom nodded and headed off to the right hand side with Claire in tow. As he reached the end of the line, he shouted to Claire.

"Stay behind me and let me know if any of them are sneaking up on us. Tap me on the shoulder of whatever side they are at. I might not hear you over the gunfire."

Claire grunted an affirmation, her throat felt too dry to speak.

Tom adjusted his stance let off the safety and began focussing on the attackers. There seemed to be dozens of them moving in the tree line. The men were firing in controlled bursts and every now and again one of the figures would race towards the skirmish line only to be hit with a hail of modified bullets. The effect on the creatures was spectacular. For a split second there would be no visible reaction then they seemed to turn to a humanoid image in ash before this would explode in a flash of orange flame and disperse to nothing. All of this within a second.

"Wow"" Tom hated that he was reduced to the simplest of exclamations but he was astonished with the impact their weapons had. He decided it was time to join in.

A creature that looked like it had been a harmless emo teenager only days before made a beeline for Tom. It came at him on all fours and launched itself over the barbed wire perimeter. Tom went into auto pilot, he controlled his breathing and aimed instinctively centring the circular sight of his gun on the chest of the vampire and fired. The machine gun gave a short sharp burp as three specially modified bullets – Tom did not know if they were ash, hawthorn, iron or silver and didn't care – thumped into the vampire's chest. For a horrible second Tom thought the bullets had no effect but once more there was the likeness to ash at the end of a cigarette then the creature blew apart. He was vaguely aware of Claire vomiting behind him then she tapped his right shoulder hard.

A vampire launched itself from one of the low hanging trees and landed inside the wire, it raced toward the water filled trench. Tom knew it should not be able to cross the stream but it was not slowing down. He aimed, pulled the trigger and was dismayed to hear a dull click rather than a burp.

"Stoppage, stoppage." He shouted, wishing he had a pistol as back up as he forced the chamber of the gun clear. He knew that he would not manage it before the creature reached him. There was a loud rip of gunfire to his left and the creature erupted in flame and vanished. Tom turned and nodded thanks to the young private who had saved his life.

The soldier gave him a brief salute then continued firing to the front. Tom cleared his gun and raised it ready to fire again but noticed the vampires were gone. Section leaders all around the perimeter could be heard shouting the cease fire order. Everyone stood to staring out into the darkness while the men on the armoured vehicles used the searchlights to cut through the darkness in a set out pattern. Pretty soon it was obvious the attack was over.

Officers and NCOs shouted for the sentries to get back in position and for the sections to form up while a roll call was carried out. Tom saw Major Blood and walked up to him, Claire followed a bit unsteady on her feet and not at all keen on her first experience of a battle. Blood seemed a bit distracted but smiled at them both.

"Good to see our police force survived."

"What should we do Major?"

"Just get some rest if you can. The other four survivors are safe in their tents and we want to do a head count of our men. It seems the vampires were testing our strength and might have tried to get a couple of us but you should be safe until morning now. We will come and wake you as planned. Now please try and rest and let us worry about this."

With that he walked away from them and stood on the perimeter looking into the forest. For a few seconds his eyes locked with those of a much older creature high up in the trees. He felt cold fingers crawling through his mind then they were gone. The trees were empty. He now knew what had happened. One of the master vampires had ordered the others to attack the camp so that it could examine the reactions of the soldiers. This was not good, this was not good at all. He turned sharply on the balls of his feet and marched back to the command tent.

Chapter 17 Time to Move Out

Tom was rudely awakened from a fitful sleep and noticed it was just beginning to get light. He recognised his waker as the private from the fire fight the previous night. It took Tom a second to realise where he was then he stretched letting out a loud groan.

"The Colonel will see you in the command tent in 5 minutes Sergeant." Once he seemed convinced that Tom was not going to roll over and go back to sleep he ran over to Claire's bed and roughly shook her awake. Claire was equally rough in her verbal response before she sat up in her camp bed and stared bleary eyed across at Tom.

"Aw crap," she muttered and ran her hand through her messy hair.

"Not a good look Claire." Tom said smiling at her discomfort. She stuck her tongue out at him and headed towards the toilets to wash up. Tom scratched his head and realised he had a serious case of dog breath and could do with brushing his teeth and a wash.

Some five minutes later both police officers were reunited in the command tent with Steven, Becky, Teresa and Father O'Reilly. Claire noticed how tired everyone looked included Colonel Forbes. They all seemed to have aged a decade overnight save for Teresa who smiled sweetly at her. Forbes explained that after the previous night's attack he wanted to personally double check everything. He went over the procedures for the two groups once more and emphasised the importance of the village group destroying all the hiding places for vampires, at this point Teresa interrupted.

"You can't burn down the chapel. God won't let you." She looked anguished towards Father O'Reilly who comforted her. Forbes leant forward across the desk and spoke in a warm soft voice to the young girl.

"Don't worry Teresa, we aren't going to burn the church. The soldiers will check it carefully and Father O'Reilly will use holy water to make sure it is safe. We both blessed some a few minutes ago." He looked towards O'Reilly as did Teresa. The old priest nodded slowly. Teresa smiled and relaxed a little. Forbes stared at her for a second, there was something strange at work with the little girl. Maybe it was just the fact that kids are more open with their imagination but he felt certain there was more to it than that. He deliberately forced the thought to the back of his mind for the moment and concentrated on matters at hand.

After ensuring the two section leaders were fully aware of what was expected, he wished them well as the two groups climbed into the back of their respective armoured personnel carriers. The drivers gunned the engines and after the rear doors hissed shut they set off in convoy along the road to Cothqon. Forbes watched them go standing at ease. He glanced up at the lightening sky noticing the red patches of sky showing through the glowering snow clouds. Red sky in the morning shepherds warning he thought to himself then looked back once more as the armoured vehicles disappeared around the bend.

"God be with you." He said and turned back towards the command tent ignoring the looks from his men manning the perimeter as he was lost in thought.

Chapter 18 A Short Journey

Claire yawned loudly inside the lead vehicle as she was bounced about on the troop bench. She felt comical with the oversized soldier's helmet messing up her hair but protecting her head from collisions with the equipment stowed inside the vehicle walls. All she could hear was the clanking of tracks and the whine of the powerful engine which competed with the churning of mud and gravel for volume. She watched Tom and Steven who somehow seemed to be managing to shout to one another above the noise. They seemed to be enjoying the ride. Boys and their toys she supposed. Major Blood or Joe as he insisted they call him sat nearest the rear door staring into space silently. He looked as though he had the weight of the world on his shoulders. Claire wondered what he knew that they didn't, but suppressed it when she realised that would only spook her further.

Joe suddenly leant forward and put a hand to his ear where a communications ear piece hung. He nodded as he spoke into it then half stood and turned to the three civilians and seven infantry men in the vehicle. He shouted loudly but still could only just be heard above the noise of the vehicle.

"That's Charlie 2, the other APC turned off into Cothqon. We are now heading onto the compound on our own. I will let you know as soon as we are nearing it."

He sat down once more and leant forward deep in thought. He felt they were taking a big risk here and he wasn't sure that civilians should be exposed. The should be safe in the armoured vehicle but would need to ensure that the compound was well defended. He just could not get rid of the bad feeling that had descended on him ever since he saw that vampire sizing up their defences last night. That wasn't the way things had went before when they had to deal with these creatures apart from the first confrontation he and Tim had many years before. He did not want to experience that sort of disaster again.

Chapter 19 Clearing Out Cothqon

Charlie two was commanded by Captain Iain Jamieson, a recent transfer from the Highlanders. Major Blood had personally briefed him on the importance of their mission and that he had to ensure the vampires were left with no hiding place whatsoever in Cothqon. This made sense to Iain. Essentially they were ensuring that they had as secure as possible communication routes between the camp and the Scottish power compound. From these strong points they could build up their strength and then fan out from those locations to reconquer the whole of the forest before assaulting the enemy stronghold at the old church. It was all solid military logic. The only thing that worried him was the same concern that Blood had. They had both seen the vampire watching the skirmish last night as though he were assessing their strength. He knew he would need to be very careful. He decided to give the men one more pep talk before they debussed.

Iain leant forward and pointed to his headphones then to the sides of the vehicle. His soldiers cottoned on immediately and pulled on the headsets hanging just above their heads and gestured for the civilians to follow suit. Once he was satisfied they were all listening Iain began.

"Okay, we all know we are entering the unknown here so we need to be careful. No one wanders on their own. We work methodically from one side of the town to the other. We search each house carefully then we torch it, plain and simple.

The only building to be left standing is the chapel but it still must be searched. The three civilians must stay in the vehicle until we reach the chapel. In the chapel Teresa and Father O'Reilly will guide us round there. We check that it is still secure then head onto the compound to reinforce Charlie One. If we follow the rules then we should be fine. Let's keep it safe and simple guys and good luck."

The men nodded in response though a couple of them looked thoughtful. It wasn't like their Captain to give pep talks and they realised he must be worried. Their thoughts were interrupted by the voice of the driver over the intercom.

"Standby to debus in five, four, three, two, one. Debus."

There was a clatter of tracks and a squeal of brakes as the APC slewed to a halt followed by the hiss of hydraulics as the rear ramp opened. Iain stepped out first with his carbine at the ready, closely followed by the rest of his section. All eight men pepper potted out from the vehicle forming a defensive cordon, the turret on the vehicle traversed a full 360 degrees.

"Anything on the sensors James?" Iain enquired into the radio mouthpiece fitted to the collar of his flak vest. There was a pause then the gunner from the turret responded.

"That's a negative sir. No life signs."

"Okay men we are good to go. We check out these 2 houses, four men to each house then work onto the next two and so on."

"Piece of cake." One of the troopers muttered to himself as they advanced towards the two semi detached houses at the end of the short street. They had main doors set to the front of the houses just off from the driveways created in their front gardens. The village seemed eerily silent, too quiet. Iain noted that there was no cawing of crows or any other sounds of wildlife which should be present in a heavily wooded area. He glanced across to the other squad of men advancing through the neighbouring garden led by Sergeant Colin "Mitch" Mitchell.

Mitch watched Iain out the corner of his eye. Colonel Forbes had asked him to keep an eye on things as he was the most experienced NCO in the whole Occult Bureau. He knew that Iain was aware he had been an officer of his rank once and was busted to the ranks and that he was aware of a special relationship between Forbes, Blood and Mitch but Mitch wasn't going to fill him in on the details. Mitch had seen this type of young officer come and go countless times in the past. Gung ho arrogant bastards too busy looking for the next promotion towards general staff to care for their men, his job was to ensure the men remained as safe as possible. Mitch was keenly aware that Iain did not like him either, he had overheard him remarking to Blood that certain classes should never become officers. That made Mitch smile as he thought of the short shrift Joe had given the man. Joe had asked where he thought he and Forbes had come from and with a sarcastic laugh had suggested that both senior officers had better watch their backs or Iain would be after their jobs. Iain didn't know it but his card was already marked. After this mission he would be returned to unit.

Mitch gestured to his earpiece and spoke into his throat mike.

"Ready to go sir. We will keep in touch if anything is in here."

"Okay Sergeant, keep your eyes peeled. Let's go." Iain answered keeping his voice professional so that his nervousness would not spread through the section. Everything seemed to be going well as his men kicked in the house door. Just get through this mission and he would have another marker on his rise to the top he told himself.

It was the third set of semi-detached houses before the soldiers saw any sign of the enemy. Mitch and his three men were crouched in the upper hallway of the left hand house and prepared to storm a bedroom each. Mitch kicked in his door and the trooper with him threw in a specially modified flash bang grenade that gave a brilliant blast of ultra violet light while the other pair did the same. Mitch entered the room and swung his gun around it. Heavy curtains covered the window so he had to rely on the torch attached to his gun to see as it cut through the darkness. The room seemed to be empty save a double bed set in the centre of it. Mitch could not ignore the obvious hiding place and ducked down to look under the bed while his partner covered him. He could hear the other pair announce loudly that their room was clear somewhere behind him and through the wall from the adjoining house he could hear Christmas music. Mitch tried to control his breathing as he reached forward to move the bed covers aside.

A maniacal face lunged out at him swiftly followed by the emaciated body of a young child. Mitch recoiled in an effort to avoid the attack but he was slightly too slow in reacting. The creature grabbed his neck with small strong hands that felt like talons. He rolled round to land on top of the vile thing that once had probably been a happy ten or eleven year old. He managed to pin the creature down while its head snapped upwards at him and spat at the other trooper. Struggling violently Mitch managed to free his silver combat knife from its leg sheath and sliced across the creature's throat several times going deeper with each stroke. With one final effort he managed to decapitate the thing and it dissolved into a heap of ashes. He pushed himself up onto his knees and took deep breaths to bring his heart under control. That was close, much, much too close for his liking. He blew out his cheeks as he looked at his comrade who watched him with concern.

"Fox, what the fuck were you doing?" He said. He slapped the ground angrily.

"I couldn't get a clear shot Mitch. I didn't want to hit you."

"What are these for?" He pointed at his armoured flak vest and shook his head in frustration while Fox visibly blushed. He knew his Sergeant was just pissed off and frightened but he still felt guilty.

"You ok Mitch?" He asked. Another soldier, Corporal McGahan came into the room looked at the pile of ashes and offered his hand to Mitch while the fourth soldier Jones looked on from the doorway.

"Got a bit close there Mitch? The rest of the house is clear. Jones and I just checked the other rooms."

Mitch accepted McGahan's hand and got to his feet. He kicked at the pile of ashes in disgust. He hated these creatures, especially when they had taken over kids. It made him think of his family. The thought that he would never see them again hit him like a hard punch in the guts and he kicked the ashes again then regained control. He was getting plenty of chances to extract his revenge on these bastards.

"Right guys, move on to the next house. We only have a few hours of daylight left. McGahan, you set the fire for here."

They left the room without looking back. McGahan nudged Fox and gave him an enquiring look. He was wanting to know what had happened but Fox just shrugged his shoulders. It wasn't worth explaining.

****

In the adjacent set of semi detached houses Jamieson led the way and slowly opened the back door to the building as he crouched on the steps with his other hand holding his gun at waist height. He willed his breathing to slow to a calmer rate and tried to make no sound as the door edged outwards revealing a dimly lit kitchen. Movement to his left caught his eye and he blinked to be sure he was seeing properly. It seemed that a mother was helping her child with something on the cooker. The mother leant across the cooker top while the little girl stood on tip toe closely watching whatever she was doing. They both had their backs to him and paid no attention to the soldiers crowded in the doorway. A radio blared out Dean Martin crooning *Let it snow, let it snow* giving the scene a surreal feel while large snowflakes landed on Jamieson's Gore-Tex smock.

He took aim looked through his optical sight and placed the top of the marker post on the centre of the woman's back. He took first pressure on the trigger but for some reason couldn't bring himself to pull fully on the second pressure. It looked such an innocent scene, he just couldn't bring himself to kill unarmed civilians.

He blinked once more to clear his eyes and to psych himself up but it was already too late. He was deafened by two short controlled bursts from the soldier alongside him.

The mother half turned at the bark of the gun but she was already turning into flaming ash. Jamieson had enough time to see her gaping mouth with razor sharp teeth as she looked in rage and anguish down at her dissolving body. The flames engulfed both creatures and all that remained were piles of greasy ash. The two soldiers entered the kitchen and checked there were no others in the room.

Jamieson stepped forward to investigate what the creatures had been looking at on the cooker. What he saw caused bile to rise up hot in his throat, he ran to the sink and vomited violently retching up all of his last meal. Out of curiosity the other soldier looked over at the cooker.

The steaming remains of a very young baby were spread out on the cooker surface. The belly had been split open and the innards were exposed giving off a small cloud of condensation in the freezing air of the kitchen. The soldier struggled to keep his own stomach in line and looked away towards the doorway to the sitting room while he waited on his superior to compose himself. He hadn't enjoyed shooting the two creatures when he wasn't certain that they were vampires but he had learnt long ago to remain cold and focussed on these operations.

Chapter 20 Arrival at the Compound

Joe gestured for everyone to hold tight as the vehicle slewed to a halt inside the compound. They heard the loud mechanical clunk click of gears slotting into place and the APC reversed slowly towards the main door of the building. Tom watched as Joe spoke into the mouthpiece of his headset.

"Any life signs on the sensors?" Tom shouted. He waited a second then the gunner's northern accent came through from the turret sounding worried.

"Not a dickie bird sir. I mean there are literally no life signs within the range of our sensors. There should at least be birds or rabbits or something."

"Okay Jones. Don't sweat it, just keep your eyes peeled while we ensure the building is secure."

The gunner seemed to have regained his composure as he responded.

"Sorry sir. Roger that. We will cover your rear."

Joe gestured for everyone to put on the headsets then once they were in place he spoke quickly for everyone's benefit.

"We are at the door of the compound. Alpha squad under my command will search the building while Bravo squad will secure the doorway and the rear ramp of the vehicle. Tom, Claire and Steven you will come with Alpha and guide us through the building. We keep in touch through the throat mikes." He gestured to the neck mikes on the flak vests they all wore including the civilians then added. "If things go tits up in the building we race back to the vehicle and leave. No excuses. Understand?"

There was a chorus of affirmative responses then they removed the headsets. The ramp lowered with a hydraulic hiss and a clang as it hit the edge of the compound building. Joe took a deep breath and raced out followed by the others with their weapons in the ready position.

Joe was glad that he had studied hand drawn plan of the buildings with Steven the day before, he was also glad that Steven had been pretty damn accurate with his drawings. With Steven typing in the code on the keypad they checked through the hydraulic main door and were in the small lobby that was similar to an airlock waiting for him to type in the second code on this keypad when Steven paused his mouth forming a perfect O.

"Oh no." He exclaimed.

"What's the matter?" Joe asked.

"Someone has been in here." Steven said in a strange distant voice. He pointed at two green flickering lights at the top of the keypad. "Those lights mean the alarm has been tripped and someone has been inside."

All of the soldiers tensed up and raised their guns as did Tom. Joe took a deep breath then clapped a hand on Steven's shoulder who visibly flinched. Joe knew the man was frightened so he wanted to ensure this was not just the result of panic. He leant towards Steven and asked quietly.

"Steven think very carefully, is it possible that this has been tripped accidentally?"

Steven's eyes looked up to the left as he thought then he shook his head.

"It can only be tripped by someone or something entering the building. I mean it could be an animal but how on earth would they get past the keypad?"

"Okay," Joe conceded, he gently pushed Steven behind him and gestured for the three troopers to come forward. "We will enter first while you come directly behind us giving us details of each room. As I said if it goes tits up run for the entrance shouting on the others. Understand?"

Steven, Tom and Claire nodded slowly, their eyes wide with fear. "Don't worry I won't hang about." Steven muttered then louder he said.

"The code is 72688474, spells out Scottish on an alpha numeric pad."

Joe nodded to his men and they covered him as he typed in the code. There was a mechanical click followed by a short slow hiss and the door opened inwards to expose the dimly lit interior. His throat dried up as he stepped over the entrance and he was certain that the temperature dropped perceptibly as they advanced scanning the corridor with their guns. He spoke softly into his throat mike.

"Okay men keep those eyes peeled and cover one another's backs. We search one room at a time and work our way through."

A series of affirmations followed.

"First room is the comms room." Steven said through his mike.

Steven waited on the edge of the first doorway covering two of his men as they swiftly entered the comms room and surveyed it. The room was empty save for the computer terminal and comms equipment which was strewn everywhere with electrical wires and circuit boards cracked and spread out across the room. Steven had a quick look at the debris and turned to the others with a look of despair.

"It's all beyond repair."

"No kidding." Quipped one of the troopers but he shut up when Joe glared at him.

"We had to expect this Steven if they got in. Don't worry though we have powerful comms in the APC. We will transfer the equipment through to here. We need to search the rest of the compound."

Steven nodded meekly and followed the soldiers along the corridor. Claire trailed along at the back of the group. She was scared but felt safer in this group of soldiers since she had witnessed them fighting the vampires the night before. She just wished she knew how to use one of the machine guns or rifles but at least she had a browning pistol to defend herself with, hopefully it would not come to that though. She glanced nervously over her shoulder but could just make out the shapes of the men guarding the entrance. *At least our backs are covered.* She thought.

It took thirty minutes for Joe's unit to search the whole compound and regroup with the guards at the entrance. They had established that there were no vampires inside and that they had achieved access through the rear of the building where a door had been ripped open. The soldiers sealed off this door with some welding gear carried in the APC and Joe used blessed holy water to ensure that vampires could not come through that way again in a hurry. They sat in a circle outside the building in a Chinese parliament under the midday sun. Joe spoke first.

"Okay, we know that they got into the compound now and wrecked the comms but everything else is intact. We need to find out how they crossed the streams. My money is on us finding one section blocked up so that they can cross dry land to here. We need to find this and remove it so the water is securing us again then we bed down here and wait on Charlie two arriving. After this we should be able to sit tight till reinforcements come through."

A couple of the troopers looked at one another so Joe spoke again.

"Come on folks we have the Chinese parliament tradition here so speak your minds."

One of the privates cleared his throat then spoke.

"Sir, we are going to be really exposed here. What happens if they send as many to attack us here as they did last night?"

Steven spoke softly at first his voice growing stronger as if his confidence were growing.

"It should be fine once we have the streams running and the perimeter secured. I stayed here when they were right outside the gate and they never got in at me."

He looked from one person to the next until he had met the eyes of everyone and they all saw the sincerity and belief in his.

Claire looked around then decided to add her tuppence worth.

"The running water should protect us and if we use holy water at any entrances we should be okay."

"I agree." Joe said. "We will bring in some of the comms equipment from the APC and we can decide whether to have them manned during the night or not. I think it should be manned but I will ask for volunteers and if we cant have any we will secure them and bed down inside the building."

"The firepower of the APC would be good but I think the men inside could be exposed if the perimeter fence is breached. Can we risk leaving any of our number exposed?" Tom asked.

"The rules of our Chinese parliaments are that everyone has a fair say Tom. Instead of me giving orders I open up the floor to everyone and a majority needs to agree on what happens. In this case if the majority decides we should be all together in the one position then that's what we do."

A few of the troopers nodded at this.

Claire raised her hand. "Do we have enough equipment and weapons to stay over night and then fight out in the morning if we need to?"

"We believe so," Joe told her. "We should have enough equipment etc for a few days. Charlie Two will join us soon too. That will double our strength in everything plus I think we have a secret weapon with them."

"Teresa?" Claire said.

Joe just nodded.

"That little girl really has something," Tom said, "I don't know what it is but she held up a cross when we were under attack in the camp and it glowed like I dunno... like a light sabre in those star wars films. It was spooky but really comforting."

Joe listened intently. He had been very interested in the priest's earlier story about the girl and her description of chasing the vampire from her home. "I have only seen one other person who could do that, Colonel Forbes. Tim got us out of a tight spot once when we were surrounded by a group of vampires. I heard that Father O'Reilly is the same as is Reverend Davidson from the Church of Scotland down the hill. Both clergy men were sent here because of this ability."

Claire felt her jaw drop at this casual revelation "So the churches knew about the vampires?"

"Yes, the churches have known about vampires for centuries but I suppose it is similar to exorcism. They don't really talk about it but they have their specialists who can deal with these particular problems. Anyway, I think we will have two people able to defeat these creatures within our group when Charlie two arrives. We can discuss this more once we have secured our perimeter."

One or two of the soldiers glanced about nervously at the trees surrounding the compound as if they expected vampires to advance towards them. Joe pointed to two soldiers and ordered them to check the perimeter together in a clockwise motion to discover how the vampires had gained entry and then picked another two to do the same in a counter clockwise motion.

Chapter 21 The Chapel

Mitch steadied himself as they prepared to enter the doorway to the chapel. He held his gun level with chest height and spoke quietly to the priest who produced a vial of holy water.

"Are you ready, Father? I will cover you but if anything comes at you just duck and I will deal with them."

Damien nodded grimly, he sprayed some holy water on the handles to the chapel and was gratified to see there was no reaction from the brass handles.

"That's a good sign Mitch." He said in his soft brogue. He tucked the vial of holy water into a pocket in his coat and produced his large silver crucifix. Slowly, carefully he pushed down the lever of the door and let it slide open inwards with a long low creak.

Low winter light crept into the main chancel of the chapel slowly illuminating the interior pew by pew until it finally settled on the altar that was still set out for a morning mass that had never been said. Damien felt a mixed bag of homesickness and regret at this scene. Well, after all he supposed the chapel of St Mary's had effectively been his home these last eighteen years as he and Bill Davidson had kept their vigil on that gateway of evil on the other side of the hill. He physically shook himself to get over the melancholy, he had a job to do. The Lord's work. Something that he along with many of the men here had trained many years for and sacrificed many of the things others took for granted so that they would be ready when the hour came. Damien was determined not to be found wanting at this time of need. He breathed in deeply of the freezing air then advanced cautiously.

The soldiers followed behind fanning out as they entered, one of them walked over to the far left wall and hit a few switches. The lights did not come on at this but Damien was not surprised he just switched on a torch and was quickly copied by everyone else. Soon beams of light were cutting arcs through the air. It did not take too long to realise that the main part of the chapel had not been touched. Damien walked up to the alter and then lifted a chalice that contained some Eucharistic wafers. "Might need these later," he commented to no one in particular as he placed the chalice in his backpack. "There are more in a cupboard in the sacristy along with more holy water that we could use."

Mitch was alongside Damien by now and looked around the altar area. He gestured for two of his men to get ready to open the door connecting the sacristy.

Damien walked over with Mitch alongside him. Damien glanced back to the chapel entrance and could see Teresa and Becky surrounded by the remaining troops just outside the doorway next to the parked APC. Teresa offered him a supporting smile which Damien returned weakly.

One of the two soldiers opened the door while the other knelt aiming inwards with his carbine. Damien held the crucifix in front of himself and was happy to see that there was not even the faintest glimmer from it. He was pretty sure they were safe here but did not want to let his guard down yet. The four of them entered the small sacristy and could see that there wasn't anyone hiding there. Damien searched the wall cupboard quickly and efficiently. He soon produced a small wooden box of Eucharistic wafers and placed these in the backpack followed by a large bottle of holy water. He glanced around the room while Mitch did the same. Mitch pointed to a heavy looking wooden door on the back wall and asked.

"Does that lead to the chapel house?"

"It actually leads outside to a short path that goes to the chapel house. The two buildings aren't physically connected. Oh…"

"Oh." Mitch nodded. "How much would you like to wager that some of the freaks are hiding out in your old house?"

"I think I would lose that wager." Damien said. "There is one way to check for certain." He added nodding to his backpack. He reached inside and brought out one of the vials of holy water. Mitch nodded his agreement slowly. He liked the old priest, he certainly had some balls. He advanced on the heavy door and spoke into his mike as he did so requesting for two more soldiers to join them.

The two other soldiers were by their side by the time Mitch opened the door slowly. As Damien had described it led onto a short path closed in on either side by tall narrow brick walls as it made its way straight as an arrow towards another wooden door set in an old stone wall. The five soldiers and priest gingerly made their way along the path, large snowflakes meandered lazily towards the ground while smaller more mobile flakes swirled around them. Damien slowly dripped holy water from the vial onto the handle of the chapel house door and waited to see how it reacted. They did not have long to wait.

Steam hissed from the chrome door knob and an acrid smell filled their nostrils. Damien turned to Mitch, his face grim as he put the vial in his back pack and pulled out the crucifix.

"Looks like we have our answer Mitch." Mitch did not answer, he raised his carbine to chest head and gestured with his head for one of the men to open the door while the others prepared to storm the house.

The knob of the door turned silently at the soldier's touch and the door slid inwards with theatrical slowness on its hinges. The soldiers shone powerful ultra violet torches into the long central hall of the house. Nothing seemed out of place.

"Okay, keep it tight lads. Eyes peeled and on your toes."

"Roger that." One of them responded. Their was palatable tension in the men as they searched the three ground floor rooms; a sitting room, a dining room and a kitchen.

So far so good Mitch thought but he knew they were here somewhere.

"Does this have a cellar or basement Damien?" He asked. The priest shook his head.

"Just this floor and the first floor along with the entire loft floored as the one room. I think they will be in the loft."

Mitch grunted his agreement and the men climbed the stairs covering one another as they went. Two of the three doors in the upper hallway were open and a quick search revealed them to be empty. The men all looked at one another as they approached the final door set at the end of the corridor.

"This is the door that leads upstairs to the loft." Damien whispered. He raised the crucifix slowly and they could all see the bright blue glow around the edges. Somewhere up above them faint noises could be heard as terrible creatures stirred from their slumber. The soldiers all raised their weapons ready to fire. Damien visibly steeled himself for the inevitable confrontation and slowly turned the door handle.

Chapter 22 Assessing the Situation

Joe sat at a table in the mess of the compound with plans of the area spread out in front of him. His men were situated around the compound securing the area or checking and stockpiling what supplies remained. He felt more comfortable now that they had discovered where the vampires had blocked off the stream and remedied the situation. He could concentrate on ensuring that once the troops from Charlie 2 arrived they were ready to survive the night and then launch further attacks in the morning. He had managed to contact Forbes and tell him that they had secured the compound and the Colonel had assured him that more troops would arrive in the morning to carry out sweeps of the forest. He looked up as he heard footsteps come along the corridor. Tom and Claire came into the mess.

Tom came towards him. "I would like permission to show Claire and Steven how to use weapons. I think that we might need all the help we can get if the vampires get back in here."

Joe thought about this for a second but he did not need to take too long. "There are extra MP5s in the APC, ask Jones and he will issue them to you with ammunition and instruct you on the best way to practice until you are ready to defend yourselves."

Tom raised a hand in a salute and they headed back out. Joe returned to working out his next move. He tapped the point on the map where the post office was with his pencil thoughtfully. It was crucial that they make contact with the forces there but he had not been able to pick up any messages from them. Tom had been correct about one thing; if they do not manage to connect with the others then they will need all the armed people they can muster. Joe believed in hoping for the best while preparing for the worst. For that very reason he had checked with his vehicle crew that the APC could be reversed up tight against the entrance so that they could escape directly from the compound buildings into the vehicle if they had to evacuate in a hurry. He pinched the bridge of his nose and tried to clear his mind of doubts, he needed a sharp mind for the night ahead.

Chapter 23 Training Day

Tom led Claire and Steven to the static APC and found Bob Jones carrying out some routine maintenance on the .50 cal machine gun. He waved a friendly greeting to them and climbed down from the roof of the vehicle landing on the snow covered ground with a dull thud.

"What can I do for you guys?" Bob enquired.

Tom took his helmet off. "Joe said you would train my colleagues here on using the spare guns in the APC. We might need all the firepower we can get tonight."

Bob nodded and grinned. "The Major knows I like trying out my instructor skills every chance I get. If he has suggested it then I consider that an order that must be obeyed." He gave an exaggerated salute and climbed into the rear of the APC. Clare liked the easy going nature of the soldier and she thought there was something attractive about him.

Bob came back carrying three guns minus their magazines to complement the one that Tom already carried over his shoulder. He also carried a satchel which Tom suspected held several magazines for the machine guns.

Bob led them round the side of the compound to an area that had been cleared for a car park. He placed the machine guns and the satchel down on a large boulder and moved two empty plastic containers about ten yards away then came back to the boulder. He put his hands on his hips and looked Claire and Steven up and down as if he were assessing them. Claire liked the air of drama he was creating then he spoke with authority while he eyeballed them.

"Okay lady and gentleman today you are going to learn how to defend yourself against attack from deadly plastic containers. I will quickly go through how you load, cock, aim and fire these weapons. The MP5 is a highly accurate and reliable sub machine gun packing a deadly punch over a short range. The bullets we use have been specifically designed to kill vampires. You hit them in the heart they die. I will train you in a short period of time to be confident that you will hit them in the heart most of the time. Hopefully after this I will feel safe fighting alongside you."

He picked up two of the sub machine guns and handed them to Claire and Steven who handled the weapons gingerly.

"It's okay," Bob said, "They don't have any bullets in them yet so just get used to the feel of the weapon in your hands, how it weighs and balances. In a moment I will give you a loaded magazine but I want you to be comfortable with the weapons. Follow what I do until it feels natural."

He started with aiming the gun at eye height and the others followed suit. For a few minutes he carried out what looked like martial arts moves aiming the gun in different directions increasing the speed of the movements until they were out of breath slightly. Bob seemed satisfied with the progress of the other two so he bent down and picked up three magazines from the satchel. He passed one each to Claire and Steven who were surprised at how heavy they were. Bob cleared his throat and said.

"We will go through how we load a magazine and cock the weapon then we will go through the routine for changing a magazine safely and quickly. I want to be satisfied you can handle this before we go onto firing at the targets."

Bob went through the routines several times with them constantly emphasising the importance of having the weapon's safety catch in place until they fired and the need to ensure that they never had the gun pointed at a person unless they intended to shoot them. After several repetitions of this he gave a demonstration of firing his weapon at the containers, shifting aim from one to the other while he emptied the thirty round magazine in three round bursts. After removing the magazine and checking that there were no rounds in the chamber he turned to Claire. "Now it's your turn. I've only shown you how to use three round bursts as we don't do full auto but want some rapid firepower so it is a decent compromise. Take aim at the left container then the right container until your magazine is empty. Take careful aim and fire when you are ready. Go."

Claire took a deep breath and aimed as she was told. When she fired she was surprised that she had aimed high. She adjusted as she turned to the right and heard the satisfying dull thud as the bullets ripped into the container. She continued until her magazine was empty managing to hit more often than she missed.

Bob patted her on the shoulder after she proved that her weapon was empty and then Steven took his turn. He carried out a similar record of hits and misses. Bob seemed happy enough with their performances. He produced several magazines that he handed to each of them. "We have some spare webbing belt kit in the APC I will give you so that you can carry the magazines for the weapons, I would suggest you wear them from now on whenever you are awake and always have the weapons on your person even in daylight." Claire and Steven then followed Bob and Tom back to the APC. They both felt a bit more confident now that they were armed and knew how to defend themselves. Bob wasn't so sure about arming civilians but if the gaffer ordered it then he must feel they would need the firepower later so who was he to argue and he understood that they could not leave anyone defenceless. Looked like it was going to be a long night ahead of them.

****

Claire sat on the bed she had lain down on the night before last. It seemed a lifetime ago now. She suddenly felt overwhelmed , and began to sob quietly as she thought of all the dead bodies she had seen and felt even worse when she thought of the creatures that the others had become. Then, she was startled as a shadow cut off the light from the doorway. She gave a huge sigh of relief to see Tom in the doorway. He entered and softly closed the door behind him. "How are you holding up?" He asked, the concern written plainly across his face. He sat down on the bed beside her and put his arm around her shoulder. She moved into his arms and let the tears surge out.

"I can't help thinking about all those poor people. Those creatures are the stuff of nightmares. It's like finding out the monster in the cupboard that terrified you as a kid actually exists."

She buried her face into his chest and Tom gently patted her back.

"You know Claire, sometimes it's okay to be scared. Christ I'm scared of these things."

Claire looked up at him, her eyes were red and bleary and her blonde locks were plastered to her cheeks. She looked so vulnerable.

"You're scared?"

"Aye, of course I am. I spent all of my career working with the certainty that everything has a scientific explanation but tonight that was turned on its head. These creatures scare the hell out of me."

Claire muttered something about them having every right to be scared.

Chapter 24 Clash of Personalities

Damien had turned the door handle slowly intending to enter the loft stealthily but Mitch kicked the door wide open and surged through the doorway followed swiftly by two of his troopers. They covered each other with their weapons while searching the darkness with the torches attached to the gun barrels. Beams of light cut through the darkness with dust motes dancing lazily within them. The Loft was much larger than Mitch had imagined with a multitude of small passageways created between piles of clutter that must have been gathered over decades.

"Shit, this is going to take a while." Mitch muttered. He clicked on his throat mike and declared.

"right guys fan out slowly but make sure you can cover one another. I need to call this one and get support. Get your flash bangs ready."

There followed a series of rogers from his men who were in the loft with him. Damien tapped him on the shoulder to grab his attention and nodded towards the crucifix in his other hand which was almost aflame with light. Mitch was about to comment when he heard shouts from the stairway below them.

"What the hell is it?" he demanded over the mike and was astounded to see his Captain storm through the doorway. Iain glared at him with barely hidden fury.

"You are supposed to report contact with the enemy to your superior officer Mitchell. We do not want mavericks in this unit."

Mitch couldn't believe this prat, here they were about to make contact with a vampires nest and for some reason he wanted to impose his authority and start a dick measuring contest. Taking a deep breath he decided to suck it up and let Joe and Tim know later that the guy wasn't going to make it as an officer with them. Holding back his anger and with only the slightest hint of disdain he said.

"Be my guest Captain. I am sure you wouldn't want to miss out on the action." Iain barged past Mitch and announced to the troops in the loft that he was now in charge. Mitch just shrugged at the despairing looks in the eyes of his men, they realised there was nothing he could do at the moment.

"Okay men spread out and search these passages, one man down each and let's keep vocal on the microphones." Iain declared.

"Sir I instructed the men to cover one another and be ready to use flash bangs…" Mitch began

"We don't need flash bangs. When I need the advice of a Sergeant I will ask for it." Iain cut in.

He was furious that this man who could not even keep a commission was trying to steal the glory of wiping out the vampires' nest. Well there was no way that he was being denied the chance to prove himself ready for promotion. Obviously the Sergeant thought this might earn him a commission again but there was no way that Iain was going to allow that. Once they cleared this up and returned to camp he would write a report that would ensure that Forbes would never promote the meddling Sergeant. Over his dead body would this man be raised back from the ranks. He threw Mitch one final glare then advanced down the passageway directly in front of him moving swiftly past Damien. The elderly priest refused to hide his annoyance at the idiot of a career officer but Iain ignored him, he couldn't understand why they were putting so much faith in voodoo religion when the situation required a military solution.

Mitch leant towards Damien and whispered.

"Forget about that tosser Damien he won't last the week. Tim and Joe already sussed him out and are looking for an excuse to bin him."

Damien smiled slightly at this but then grew serious as he pointed to the crucifix which still glowed insanely. Mitch was deeply worried about that but all he could do was hang back at the rear protecting the priest.

"Be careful guys." He whispered as he watched his men vanish into the passageways but not before several of them had looked anxiously towards him. He held his gun at chest height ready to fire and waited for the combat to begin. He did not have long to wait.

"Holy shit! There are loads of them." Exclaimed one of the soldiers over the radio.

"I see them." Confirmed another. This was followed shortly by a high pitched screech from that far end of the loft then automatic gunfire erupted and muzzle flashes burst through the darkness.

"Get towards the door." Mitch shouted and pushed the priest behind him but Damien shook his head in refusal.

"It's too late Mitch." He raised his crucifix to face height. The cold blue light from it flickered with the intensity of a dying star bathing them in strobe light luminosity. Two soldiers came back towards them retreating slowly while firing their weapons further into the room. They finally reached the two men and all four of them formed a cordon near the doorway.

Mitch could make out the shapes of several people advancing on them from three or four directions. He checked his safety catch was off and selected his targets and began firing. The vampires that had once been villagers of Cothqon raced towards them without any organised strategy so the soldiers were able to cut them down without too much trouble but it was difficult to tell how many of them were in the room. Suddenly one diverted from the advancing group waving his arms and screaming something. Mitch was about to bring the creature down when Damien nudged his arm shouting,

"It's the Captain. Don't shoot."

It was then that Mitch realised the Captain was shouting that they shouldn't shoot. The men adjusted their aim to hit targets around the Captain who headed out the door and down the stairs. Two creatures split from the main group and managed to push past the soldiers before racing down the stairs. Mitch was torn between chasing them and finding out what happened to his men. He quickly spoke into his mike

"Two vampires have escaped and are following the Captain."

He received a roger from the Corporal in charge of the cut off force downstairs.

"Okay we need to deal with the vampires up here and find Jones and Fox."

The three soldiers and priest advanced slowly against the remaining vampires. There were only three left now and they seemed to be confused by their surroundings making it easy for the soldiers to finish them off. They heard shooting down below them and Damien lifted the crucifix and was relieved to see that the glow was beginning to die down.

Climbing over the ash remains of the defeated vampires they soon found Jones and Fox. Both men lay near one another facing opposite directions in similar condition. Their throats had been torn apart and their faces were covered in slashes. Smoke still rose from the barrels of their guns and spent cartridges glinted against the torchlight all round them. They were also covered in the ash of vampires they had destroyed. They had given a good account of themselves but Mitch was livid to lose two experienced soldiers when it could have been avoided. He knelt down and removed the dog tags from the men while the other soldiers removed any kit and ammunition that could be salvaged from them along with their guns. Mitch tapped the rapidly cooling bloody cheeks of Jones and Fox privately promising that he would make Iain pay for getting them killed and then running from the battle. He felt a firm hand on his shoulder and looked up to see Damien looking down at him with deep concern.

"I will give them their last rites."

Mitch nodded and he and the two other soldiers stood guard while the priest carried out the ritual.

A few minutes later Mitch stood outside the chapel at the rear of the APC. He watched the chapel house burn due to the incendiary devices his men had set and radioed Major Blood with the news while the medics applied emergency first aid to Iain who had been badly mauled by the two vampires that had followed him down the stairs.

****

Joe sat at the desk in the comms room staring at the ceiling in deep thought as Mitch spoke.

"We got jumped sir. There seems to have been at least a dozen of them nesting in the loft of the chapel house. We have two dead and two wounded. Fox and Jones were killed in the loft so I burnt their bodies when we torched the house. Captain Jamieson and Becky are both seriously wounded. They are being patched up and we will head towards you immediately."

"Okay Mitch - just get everything organised and we will see you soon. We have the compound secured so we can go over things when you arrive. I will report this to the Boss and find out if he wants us to change plans due to this. By the time you arrive we will know what we need to do. Is the chapel the only building remaining?"

"Yes sir. Everything else has been burnt to the ground. Damien checked it again before we torched the chapel house and it is still secure. They seem to be afraid of it. Sir."

"Okay at least that is some good news. Get your men over here ASAP."

"Roger that sir." Came the response followed by static.

Chapter 25 An Update

Joe looked up from the Comms desk at the crowd who had gathered in the room. He noticed that the police officers were also there and that Steven was hanging around in the corridor. He stood up sharply and raised his voice.

"I want everyone in the mess room in two minutes."

Shortly afterwards Joe looked around the assembled group to check that everyone was present. He took a slow deep breath to compose himself. "Most of you will have heard Mitch's report on the radio. We have lost two men and we have two people wounded. Fox and Jones. They were good men but they were volunteers like all the rest of us. This is a dangerous situation and there is a high chance that more of us perhaps all of us wont make it out of here alive. I know that isn't a pleasant thought but we must face up to the fact that here and now we are at war with a deadly enemy that will show us no mercy. We need to have the same ruthlessness as them and we must be strong." He looked pointedly at the civilians..

"I am genuinely sorry that you Tom, Claire and Steven have ended up here with us but by bad luck you have become involved. I will talk with the Boss about what we do tomorrow but we will secure us all here for tonight when Charlie two arrives. We will look at the casualties who arrive with them but there is a chance they will die before the night is over."

He checked the faces of his audience and was glad to see that even though quite a few showed signs of fear they all had a determined look about them.

" We managed to inflict a defeat on the vampires today but took casualties doing this. They will want revenge for this so there is a high chance that we will come under attack tonight so we must be prepared. Okay I just wanted to make sure everyone knew the score so get back to your duties and I will work things out with the Boss."

With this parting shot Joe marched smartly back to the comms room to talk with Forbes.

Chapter 26 The Boss is Informed

Forbes sat in his command tent while all around him men rushed to and fro carrying equipment to trucks and armoured vehicles. One of his adjutants signalled to him that a radio call was coming in for him so he picked up the headset and listened as Joe spoke.

"Charlie one for Sunray is that us through over?"

"Roger that Charlie one this is Tim you are clear to talk Joe."

There was a pause as Joe obviously collected his thoughts then Forbes listened carefully as he was brought up to speed on the clash at the Chapel house in Cothqon and the casualties sustained. He scribbled down on a notepad as he listened

Forbes nodded. "It seems that we have contacts all along the area Joe. I spoke with Charlies three and four a few minutes ago. They had clashes at the post office and at an isolated farmhouse to the South East of the university dig. Fortunately they didn't sustain any casualties and they managed to kill all the vampires they found there. It looks like we have managed to contain them but I still think we have to use the honeypot tactics so you will need to sit tight tonight. Do you have all the resources you need?"

A few miles away Joe scratched his beard thoughtfully, he could do with more men and firepower but he knew the Boss had everything allocated. "We'll manage. We will batten down the hatches once Charlie two arrives. We should have plenty of firepower to last the night."

"Ok. One more thing, inform Mitch that I have received authority to give him his old commission back. He is a Captain once again."

"He will be delighted to hear that Tim."

"I'm sure he will. Listen our met guys have told us that another storm is on its way here so comms might go down for a wee while and the Supers won't be able to get airborne so you might have to hunker down on your own for a time. We will have forces come up through the sectors that Charlies three and four are covering in the morning to relieve you. Good luck Joe."

Forbes took the headset off and looked at the rapidly dismantling camp around him. He felt a tug of guilt at not having told his friend he was pulling further back but he had to keep him convinced the battle was going to plan. A radio operator took the radio from him and carried it over to an APC. A sergeant came running over and said.

"Super one alpha is ready to take you now sir."

"Thanks Sergeant. Make sure you all get back to the fall back position before last light."

"I will do sir."

Forbes tightened the chin straps on his helmet and put his day sack over one shoulder as he marched sharply to the waiting Blackhawk where two men knelt with their minimi machine guns trained outwards while the rotors chopped the air above them. He cast one eye up the mist capped mountain then jogged the final few yards and jumped into the troop cabin of the helicopter followed by his protection squad. The helicopter lifted swiftly into the freezing air.

It didn't seem long before the second APC came racing across the bridge sliding from side to side as it entered the compound. Two soldiers raced out and closed the gate behind it as the APC turned and slewed to a halt with the rear door facing the building.

As soon as the ramp at the back of the APC lowered Mitch and Corporal McGahan climbed out before the door had even hit the ground. Bob came running forward to greet them and Mitch pointed to the interior of the vehicle.

"Bob we have two badly wounded in the vehicle they need isolated and checked over. I need to see the gaffer."

Bob gestured to another two soldiers who came running towards him while Mitch and McGahan marched smartly into the compound building. Mitch unfastened and removed his helmet and McGahan followed suit as they followed directions from their colleagues in the building until they found Joe sitting at a table in the mess eating a bowl of soup. He looked up from his snack and nodded for them to sit down opposite him. Chewing on a piece of bread he dabbed at his lips with a paper towel not quite managing to remove all the tomato stains.

"Leave us." He said without looking away from the two new arrivals. The two guards behind him left the mess room and Joe followed them closing the door before coming back to his seat. He placed the paper towel carefully on the table before barking.

"What the fuck happened at the chapel house Sergeant?"

Mitch and McGahan glanced at one another but remained silent, they were unsure how to answer so Joe continued.

"I assume that Jamieson messed up? You can both speak in confidence."

Mitch looked at the ground for a second *fuck it* he thought.

"Yes sir Jamieson messed up royally. He insisted he take over when I was ready to clear the loft and ordered that I stay out of it. He spread the men out further than I would have and they couldn't give supporting fire to each other. We were ambushed as soon as we were separated enough for the vampires to charge us. That was when he panicked."

"He cut and run sir." McGahan interjected. Mitch gave him a look that silenced him.

"He ran?" Joe checked.

Mitch nodded sadly.

"He ran Joe, leaving us fighting the vampires. Two followed him and attacked him and Becky leaving them badly wounded. McGahan and the others downstairs managed to kill them."

"He turned yellow on us." It was a statement from Joe not a question "I think Becky is going to die Joe but there's worse news." Mitch said looking at McGahan who added.

"I saw one of the vampires bleed onto Jamieson sir. Then the little girl managed to destroy it with a stake. She and Father Damien are something else, the vampires are terrified of them."

"Shit." Joe muttered. He looked from one NCO to the other then asked. "Are you certain?"

"Yes sir. It was a female vampire. She was already bleeding when she snapped at his throat and pulled his mouth open before letting her blood drip in. He tried to spit it out but he must've swallowed some."

"You both know what that means." Joe said grimly.

"I have an idea though Joe. It is risky but we could use Jamieson to see what the master vampire is up to."

Joe reckoned that Mitch had a good point, they knew from previous missions that when victims were first changing into vampires they began to have a telepathic link with the master of their nest. It was just possible that they could find out from Jamieson where the master vampire was and what he was planning. He decided to go with it.

"All right, we will use him but the minute he turns fully we need to slot him. No hesitation at all. It's risky guys because the link isn't one way. If Jamieson can see through the master's eyes then he can see through Jamieson's"

"Aye but what can he see? We both saw him counting our guns last night Joe. He will see that we are well armed and are in the compound. He already knows that or will once he wakes up. I thought the plan was that we should draw them in on us anyway?"

Joe pondered this for a second or two.

"Okay we go with it then Captain."

"I'm sure it will work Joe," Mitch began then he realised what his superior had said.

"Did you just?"

A smile spread across Joe's face, one of the few genuine moments of joy he had felt on this mission.

"Absolutely Mitch. You are in the officer class once more. McGahan here will need to salute you again."

McGahan nudged Mitch then saluted him with a mock sigh. Mitch shook his head in disbelief.

"Thank you Joe."

"Don't thank me, it was the Boss that gave you the commission. We also need a Sergeant for your section so that means a promotion for you McGahan."

It was now McGahan's turn to look surprised but he reacted quicker than Mitch returning a smart salute to both officers.

"Thank you sir."

Joe waved off the gratitude and became serious.

"Okay we need to make the compound fully secure. The men from Charlie One have secured any breaches in the perimeter and have got the stream running again so once we lock ourselves in here we will be as safe as we can be."

"Apart from being somewhere miles from here." Mitch muttered.

"Yeah but we are where we are lads. We will withdraw into the building and have one of the APCs reversed right up to the entrance so that we have an escape route. I think that once we do this we use Jamieson to find out what they are up to then we sit tight till morning. In the morning we should be able to meet up with the units down at the post office and clear out the university dig area. Once that's done we can hopefully head back to base and some home comforts."

"Sounds like a plan." Mitch commented. McGahan nodded his agreement. Joe wished he felt so confident but he needed to seem that way for the sake of his men.

"Right Mitch I need you to have Becky checked. You know what to do if she is dying. I want a close protective guard for Damian and Teresa, I have a feeling that they might just be our secret weapon in this fight. They seem to have the same powers as the Boss. After that get everyone back in the building and have Charlie one reversed up against the building with Charlie two close to the side of it. We don't have long till darkness and I don't want anyone caught outside."

The two men were about to leave when Joe signalled for them to wait.

"You forgot about your new rank badges." He looked at Mitch. "Give McGahan your slide and take Jamieson's."

"Yes sir." Came the response as the other two men snapped to attention and left to tend to their duties. Mitch took the small patch slide with the sergeant stripes from the front of his smock and handed it to McGahan as they walked.

Chapter 27 More Deaths

Bob was staring down at the body of Becky in despair when Mitch returned, he jumped slightly at the touch of his superiors' hand on his shoulder.

"Has she passed away Bob?"

He nodded grimly. Mitch looked down at the lady's pallid face framed by her dull hair as she lay on the stretcher on top of the snow. He felt saddened at the way the poor woman had died but they still had a job to do.

"Unfortunately mate, we need to deal with her body in the proper manner. It's a horrible job but ..."

He let the sentence hang in the air. Bob patted him on the back and gestured for the two medics to help him take Becky's body towards the perimeter fence where they had already prepared a space for burning. They busied themselves gathering some kindling from the trees within the fence and preparing a flamethrower while the elderly priest hurriedly carried out the last rites on her for the second time. It gave Mitch a strange comfort to see the priest carry out a ceremony he had witnessed countless times before, he almost felt the presence of God every time he saw the rites.

Mitch turned away from this and looked in the rear of Charlie Two where McGahan was organising the removal of Jamieson on his stretcher to the interior of the building. McGahan smiled slightly at him as they worked on the delirious Captain.

Mitch leaned in and took the Officers smock. He removed the rank slide from it and placed it on his own smock. He had wanted his own rank back but not this way, even though Jamieson was an arsehole he didn't deserve what would happen to him over the next twelve hours or so. He shook his head sadly as he replaced the smock in the APC and then left for the main building he had much to do.

Chapter 28 Settling Down for the Night

Darkness fell quickly this far north in the British Isles in winter and it seemed like no time had passed before the beleaguered passengers of Charlies one and two were battened down inside the Scottish Power compound. They had Charlie One reversed up against the compound with the ramp opened up into the entrance. Nothing could squeeze in the minute gap and it offered them a last escape route if needed. The light sensitive bulkhead floodlights had come on as soon as twilight had passed and the alarm sensors were operational. All of the people inside the compound were organised into different duties and they were all armed and alert. Joe felt that he had covered everything and apart from anything else keeping the troops busy would stop them fretting over the situation they were in. He had total faith in them as they had mostly served with him using honey pot tactics in various small wars but this was a completely new enemy for most of them. Having run through his checklist of duties for the men he decided to see how Mitch was doing with Jamieson.

Mitch sat back to front on a mess chair at the end of a long table. Three other armed soldiers sat in the room with him while Damian had insisted that he be present as well. All of them were watching Jamieson who was tied tightly to the table with his head propped up on some pillows. Every now and again one of the soldiers leant forward and wiped Jamieson's brow with a cool wet cloth. His head was soaking with sweat and his eyes stared upwards without focus, he seemed to be burning up as colour rushed to his cheeks. He muttered incoherently to himself but Mitch knew that somewhere in there what remained of Jamieson could understand their questions and it was only a matter of time before they got sense out of him. He had a quick look across at the priest who hung around the entrance to the room playing absently with his rosary beads. In his travels with the army and the occult bureau in particular Mitch had seen many things that could turn your hair white overnight but he had never experienced the effect first hand of powers that Damian and Teresa had until today. Like all of the men he had heard that the Boss had such powers but he had never seen him in action. He wondered what it was like to have such strength and such responsibility.

Joe came into the room. "How is he doing Mitch?"

Before he could say anything Damian answered for him.

"He will turn any second now."

"How do you know?"

"Can't you feel the temperature dropping? That isn't due to nightfall it's due to him." He nodded towards the stricken officer and stopped playing with his rosary. The certainty in his voice horrified Joe.

Jamieson's eyelids flicked open and his head rose from the pillows. Cold, furious silver discs had replaced the officer's human eyes and these surveyed the men in the room. Joe noticed that his exhaled breath was curling tenders of vapour in front of him now.

Jamieson or what remained of him hissed while the eyes flicked from man to man sizing each of them up. The men were chilled to the bone when the creature started to speak in sibilant tones.

"Ah the warriors and the shaman think they can spy on me? You are like children sitting at my knees. Young disobedient children. Why didn't you run while you could children? Now it's too late. Much, much too late."

The creature laughed at its own humour, a cruel mirthless laughter that could make men go insane. Joe could feel the ancient instincts deep inside his mind screaming at him to run from this obscenity. Humans have no reason to meddle with this kind of power it howled. The creature sharply turned its eyes onto him. He could feel icy tentacles grope their way into his mind as he sank deeper into those silver pools of eyes. From somewhere inside his head he heard a slick soothing voice convince him that everything would be fine that the master had a special place for brave warriors like him. Some of the others would need to die and that was a pity but the master only wanted the strong. The strong of body could lead his children when they hunted while the strong of mind could work out strategies for dealing with this modern world. The master was all powerful and all seeing but he had slumbered for a long time and he needed modern thinkers to help him adjust. Joe could feel a part of his mind turn traitor and accept these soothing promises. Yes, it promised he would serve the master and yes it would make sense that he should join a powerful leader.

Joe struggled more shaking his head violently. From a great distance it seemed he heard an old voice shouting. An argument seemed to be going on in another room, a particularly violent argument. He felt a hard slap and thought he was literally seeing stars. When his eyes began to focus he was convinced that Damian had a halo round his head but as they focussed fully he realised this was the diffusion of the fluorescent lights behind his head.

"Don't look into his eyes Joe for the love of God don't look into his eyes."

He shook his head to clear it then looked at the creature but was careful not to make eye contact.

The creature threw back its head howling in mocking laughter. It seemed to find this all hilarious.

"Ah the witch doctor breaks my spell. Come come shaman why don't you challenge me directly? My people tell me that you are very much the hero. They are a little scared of you but they are just beginning their life as a vampire. I will enjoy testing my powers against yours Damian."

The eyes widened as Damian started at the use of his name.

"Oh yes I know your name Damian. Do you think that when I was slumbering that I was ignorant of events around me? I knew of the attempts by previous warriors to raise me when that idiot from Austria threatened here. They tried to kill me and failed just like you will fail. Where is the little one?"

The men were all caught out with this change of tact and looked at one another so the creature raised its voice.

"Where is the child that has the gift of light? My people tell me that there is one among you. She will make a great servant. I always enjoy taking the life blood of the innocent. Their fear makes them taste divine."

Another cackle from the creature as it laughed at its own vile humour "What's wrong priest? No sense of humour? Oh the fun we will have when we meet in person."

Damian had heard enough, he stepped forward and planted the cross from his rosary in the centre of the creatures head and roared.

"Begone vile creature from this child of God! In the name of our Lord Jesus Christ I banish you!""

The skin on the creature's head began to pucker up and blister as steam rose around the area the cross touched. The creature howled in pain for a few seconds then cackled as the steam began to dissipate and the skin smoothed out.

"You need to try better than that shaman." The creature hissed, a long grey tongue slipped put of the mouth and flicked across two razor sharp canines before the mouth opened wide and a howl of anguish erupted from it.

No-one had noticed Teresa come into the room. She had the same trance like expression on her face the soldiers had seen before back in the village and a glow spread down her arm towards the small silver cross she thrust into the vampire's left cheek. She muttered something that Damian would later explain was a psalm in Latin and pushed the cross deeper into the cheek.

"This isn't possible, we destroyed you all." The vampire roared its voice significantly higher pitched now as an edge of fear crept in amongst the rage. A slight smile lifted the edge of Teresa's mouth as her eyes remained vacant. She enjoyed the feeling of power as God worked through her. Slowly step by step the master vampire withdrew from Jamieson's body until he was gone completely and Jamieson's head flopped back onto the pillow. Teresa slumped slightly and Mitch helped her back out of the room towards one of the bedrooms.

Joe was concerned for her but realised she had given them the opportunity to look though Jamieson to see where the creature was hiding.

Damian put his rosary beads into Jamieson's hand and Joe spoke softly to him. "Iain what can you see? If you are still in there you should be looking through the master's eyes. What is he doing?"

Jamieson had his eyes closed, they moved left to right under his eyelids as if he were dreaming and he spoke in a slurred voice. "We are in a dark tunnel I'm not sure where. There are a few vampires around, one of them is an older bald man. The master calls him teacher and he is telling him to work out a way to get in here. The master is very angry and is demanding that the vampires make an assault tonight without delay. The teacher is arguing that they need a little time to check where our defences are weaker but the master is telling him that he has fought in many battles and knows how to judge defences. He wants to inspect them personally and wants the forces ready within the hour."

He paused and went perfectly still for a second and Joe thought he had fully converted to a vampire but then he continued. "I think they are in a church crypt or something. Hang on there are tools all over the place, I think it is the archaeology site. I'm certain it is. They seem to be sitting next to a culvert that looks like a dry stream bed and there is a large iron cross in the corner. They are all avoiding that corner and some of them are moving to and fro. Oh no they have some live people down there hanging from the walls, some of the vampires are feeding from them. I can't make out who they are but there seems to be at least a dozen of them hanging there. There is something strange. I can see what the master is thinking while the others can't. He is keeping something from the others, I think he wants the attack as a distraction so that he can…Oh God he knows I'm here."

Jamieson let out a horrific high pitched scream that caused Joe and Damian to recoil from him. He sobbed pathetically then suddenly went still.

"What do you think Joe?" Mitch asked, he eyed Jamieson with concern then turned back to Joe. Damian took back his rosary beads back and felt Jamieson's skin, it was freezing cold. He shook his head sadly at the loss of yet another soul to these vile creatures.

Joe rubbed his eyes to chase away some of the fatigue that was overwhelming him. "I think we give him a little while longer. We might get one more chance at seeing what the master is doing then we will deal with him."

Damian shook his head. "I don't think we should risk that Joe he is already very cold and we can't trust them once they have gone cold. It would be like having a fox in the hen house." He shrugged as he said this last.

Joe looked up from his seat to make eye contact with the priest.

"I know where you are coming from Damian but we need to take every advantage we can get. If we have two guards on him and he is fastened down with cords dipped in holy water it should be okay."

He stared at Damian a second longer than was absolutely necessary to get the point across that this was not up for discussion. The priest simply shrugged once more in response and walked out of the room guiding Teresa by her shoulder to go with him.

"That could've gone better." Mitch muttered. Joe nodded his agreement.

"I want a permanent guard on Jamieson, never less than two men. I don't want him being able to do that hypnosis trick on any individuals. If one of you needs to take a piss or anything you have someone come in to take over your post before you go out of the room."

"No problem." Mitch responded. "I think we have enough men here to have three guarding here at all times. At what point do we slot him? I mean when do we know it's the right moment?"

Joe moved to his feet, the chair scraping across the linoleum floor. "I will question him once more in about an hour and then you can deal with him. From what he described I can't imagine them attacking us before then. It sounded like he was still rallying his troops just now. Keep frosty, I'm going to try and get a little rest before things kick off. If I don't call back within the hour give me a shout."

"Will do." Mitch agreed. Joe headed off towards the luxury of a comfortable bed for what he knew would probably be minutes rather than hours. Something that

Jamieson had said worried him, it worried him deeply. What could the master be using the attack as a decoy for? What was he planning to do? Joe started to realise that the one fatal flaw in a honey pot tactic was that the enemy might overrun you while they still have enough force to carry out their own plans at the same time.

****

It felt like he had just let his head hit the pillow when Joe jumped alert, the klaxon alarms were blaring inside the compound and he could hear the thudding of running feet in the corridors. He rubbed his bleary eyes and gave his head a rough shake to try and clear his mind before the inevitable arrival of his men looking for updated orders. He kicked his feet over the edge and stood up. Years of soldiering had left him with the habit of keeping his boots on so he just needed to grab his webbing kit and carbine to be ready to rock and roll. He had clicked together the fastening clips on his belt when McGahan came racing in almost colliding with him.

"'We're under attack. They are launching things at the perimeter fence and trying to block the stream. We are holding them off so far but there are loads of them. Mitch sent me to get you while he has rushed to organise the troops."

Joe rushed out of the door ensuring the sling of his carbine held it steady across his chest so he could bring it quickly up to an aiming point. He already had his parka smock on so he didn't need to wrap up before venturing outside. He was a bit annoyed that the men had obviously moved the APC but he knew that Mitch would have thought it through. He marched swiftly along the corridor towards the door then had a thought as he moved.

"McGahan, make sure there are at least three men guarding Jamieson and then check on the civvies. We are going to need them especially Teresa before the night is over."

With this he went outside where at last the alarms started to have to compete for attention with the noise of gunfire. It was strange for him yet again to see bodies hurl themselves at bullets in the middle of a blizzard which restricted the visibility even though the bulkhead lights on the building were very powerful. Joe took a second to orient himself then recognised Mitch walking up and down the skirmish line of troops near the gate barking orders to the men. Controlled shots of bullets surged at a crowd of vampires who were rushing towards the fence. Above all this the 50 cal machine guns on the APCs burped there cacophony of violence ripping the vampires apart.

He marched up to Mitch and shouted above the noise. "Looks like you have this under control!."

Mitch was slightly startled to see Joe next to him but recovered quickly.

"Yes sir, It feels a bit like last night though. It's as if they are counting our guns again."

"Any sign of the old guy from last night?"

Mitch shook his head. "I have been using the night vision goggles to search the tree line but I don't think he is here. I think if he was I would be able to feel his presence, you know?"

Joe nodded, he knew exactly what his friend meant. It felt similar to last night but not quite as threatening for some reason. He patted Mitch on the shoulder fondly. "Ok Mitch I'm going to check on the civvies and Jamieson. If things get too hot pull back inside and make sure whoever's in Charlie one pulls it back to cover the entrance again."

Mitch gave a thumbs up so Joe headed back indoors. He couldn't shake off the bad feeling that this was the diversion that Jamieson referred to.

Chapter 29 Fox in the Chicken Coop

McGahan had checked in the bedrooms and was happy to see that the police officers were sitting talking with the priest and Teresa calmly while keeping themselves all wrapped up in quilts to stay warm. Satisfied with this he marched onto the mess and broke into a run when he heard shouts.

Bob Jones had been assigned guard duty on Jamieson with two of his colleagues but had needed a pee so he wandered off to the toilets and left the two other troopers guarding the vampire. It was at the moment that he entered the toilets at the far end of the building that the creature came under the control of the master vampire once more. Inside what remained of Jamieson's mind he accepted that the master ruled him now and listened to what the master wanted him to do. He slowly raised one eyelid and had a sly scan of the room noting that the two troopers were not paying attention to him. They were too busy talking about the relative merits of Claire to keep vigilant and their guns were over their shoulders, this would be too easy.

One of the troopers dropped a coin he was playing with and bent down to retrieve it making the mistake of being too close to Jamieson. That was all the chance he needed. He ripped the bands that held him to the table and lunged at the nearest trooper. The second trooper rapidly unslung his carbine and brought it up to aim but Jamieson had already slashed his colleagues throat with his shiny new fangs and relished the splash of hot steaming blood. He used the dying trooper as a shield his flak vest absorbing the fusillade as the second trooper fired a short burst. Jamieson then threw the body at him and jumped upwards bursting through a grille and into the air conditioning system just as McGahan burst in. The second trooper fired a burst after Jamieson but he was already gone.

"Shit, shit!" McGahan exclaimed. He pointed at the trooper's body and ordered the other trooper to check him for any vital signs even though it was obvious he would have to be torched soon enough and then got onto the personal comms round his neck.

"Joe, Mitch. This is McGahan we have a problem in the mess. Jamieson has escaped and he has killed Schultz by the looks of it." He let out a long, low groan. Aw shit!."

Joe was half way to the mess when the call came through on the comms. He shouted into his mouthpiece as he picked up the pace.

"Mitch, I have this. You keep the perimeter intact as long as you can then fall back as agreed. McGahan I'm on my way. Secure the area as best you can."

Bob was in the toilets when the gunfire broke out. He now regretted having decided to have a crap while he was in. He quickly pulled up his combat pants and fumbled with the belt when a strange noise above him caught his attention. He had just enough time to look up and realise he was in trouble.

The air conditioning grille above him crashed down onto his head knocking him back onto the toilet pan. He struggled to free himself from the metal grille and was reaching for his gun but he had only managed to bring it close to him as strong hands grabbed him up into the darkness above. He felt hot razors slice into his exposed neck and shoulder in a frenzy while rancid breath filled his nose. Struggling a little further he managed to bring the sub machine gun to aim in a hurry and squeezed tight on the trigger. The blast of the gun was horrendous in the tight space and momentarily blinded Bob. He felt the powerful hands let go and fell through the air to the floor of the toilets landing in a heap on top of the smashed air conditioning grille. He aimed his gun upwards but the creature that had attacked him was gone.

"Shit, Shit!" He muttered to himself as he felt the blood flow from his neck and shoulder. He knew that he hadn't swallowed any blood from the creature but he also knew that he was a marked man. He quickly ran over his options within his head and decided he needed to tell his superiors what had happened. They would find out eventually anyway.

Chapter 30 Charlies Three and Four

Charlies three and four were similar APCs to those at the Scottish Power compound. Captain James Burke was the experienced commander of this unit. He had almost as much service as Joe Blood but was a gruffer man than him and tended to follow his orders to the letter. For these reasons he was not so popular with his men but they followed his orders without question as they knew he would never veer even an inch from what the Boss wanted. For this reason Corporal Andy McDowall hadn't given it a second thought when he had been ordered to drive the elderly couple from the Post Office away from the quarantine zone down to the A701 and put them on a bus for Dumfries nor did he complain about his present duties.

Andy now stood on checkpoint duty with one of his colleagues Davy Dixon they were sitting in one of two land rovers that had followed the APCs to the cut off point of the access road near the old post office. While the others were hunkered down inside the armoured vehicles they sat in the cab of their 4x4 with the heater going full blast but it didn't seem to stay within the confines of the vehicle for long. Davy sat in the driving seat his gloved hands on the huge steering wheel staring absently at the cloud of breath rising in front of him while Andy looked at the small screen showing all the sensors laid out in a picket line.

"Feels a bit exposed here Andy." He commented in his lilting borders accent.

"Yeah," Andy agreed. He was concentrating on the snaking route of the road below them, he thought he had seen lights on it but wasn't certain. "Just keep alert mate and keep the engine running."

"What is it?" Davy asked.

"Thought I saw a cars headlight down there a second ago. Better put our lights on."

Davy followed his instructions and squinted into the blizzard. Andy checked his rifle was loaded and prepared to climb out as he saw the lights once more a little bit further up the hill from earlier. Davy looked at him in alarm.

"You aren't climbing out are you?"

"Have to mate. How else will these idiots know they need to turn around?"

"Hello?" Davy remarked pointing at the bonnet of the vehicle. "This Land Rover is blocking the road and we can shout out at them."

"No that will alarm them too much. If I stop them and tell them there has been an army truck accident they will go back the way they came."

"Aye and probably say it must be a nuclear convoy." Davy retorted.

"That's better than the truth mate. Cover my back and keep an eye on the sensors."

Andy stepped out into the snow, immediately sinking a couple of inches as he walked round to the centre of the road. He held his rifle close into his chest and switched on the torch attached to his breast pocket as the approaching vehicle turned the corner in front of him. He could see that it was a civilian 4x4 and it slowed noticeably now. The occupants must have seen him and the army Land Rover and the drivers window zipped down as Andy approached waving his hand. The occupants were a middle aged couple wrapped up in Gore-Tex jackets and fleeces. *At least they are prepared for the weather.* Andy thought. He leant forward to speak to the man who drove and felt the welcome warm air from the interior.

"I need to ask you to turn around please folks. One of our trucks that was taking part in an exercise has crashed further up the road. No one can get over the mountain till we get it removed and get the injured to hospital."

The lady in the passenger seat leant across, concern written all over her face as she spoke in a north east accent. "Oh dear. Is there many hurt son?"

"Just a couple Ma'am none of them too bad but we need to have our Military Police check out the scene to ensure it wasn't careless driving. As I said we need you to turn around now. The area should be cleared in the next twenty four hours or so."

The driver nodded. He looked at either side of the road. "I'll need to do a three point turn son but we will get out of your hair right now."

Gunfire caused all three of them to turn round. A swift moving figure knocked Andy aside just before it burst into flames and ash while another dove through the open window of the 4x4. Andy was stunned for a second and as he recovered his senses he realised why he felt damp, he was covered in the blood from the driver. A pair of denim clad legs hung out the 4x4 window kicking wildly as the creature attempted to get further into the vehicle. The female passenger tried to help her husband at first but rapidly realised this was futile. She opened the passenger door and jumped out straight into the arms of a waiting vampire. She didn't stand a chance.

Andy swung his rifle round and from his seated position he let rip with a burst of 5.56mm. He saw the creature's legs stop thrashing as it realised what was happening then it flashed into flames and disintegrated. He coughed to clear his lungs of the vile ash then ran round the other side of the 4x4. Before he could get there he heard two short bursts of automatic fire and saw Davy illuminated by the brief flash of the vampire before it blew apart and the female passenger's limp body slid down to collapse at an awkward angle in the snow. Davy swung round with his gun at the aim position to face Andy as he rounded the idling vehicle. He visibly relaxed and exhaled.

"Shit, Andy! I nearly fired there."

Andy raised one hand to placate his companion then looked around in agitation. "Did you see many of them on the sensors? Do you think there are more around here?"

Davy shrugged slightly.

"The screen blurred a bit I think these were all there were but there could have been more."

The two soldiers looked at one another for a second longer then raced back to their vehicle. As they did so they didn't notice dark shapes move swiftly and silently in the direction that the civilians had come in an adjacent field. The master smiled at his old female companion, a silent message passed between them. They had escaped the warriors.

Andy turned the small screen around to face him as he climbed into the military vehicle. For a brief second he thought that a pair of smalls blip moved with impossible speed on the edge of the screen but then they were gone and the screen was completely clear. He rubbed his eyes and then decided he must be seeing things due to lack of sleep.

"I'll clear the vehicle from the road and put their bodies in it while you cover me Davy. I'll torch it while you radio into Burke. Tell him that some might've broken through our cordon. Hopefully we will get relieved by some other sad bastards so we can get a heat in one of the APCs."

He patted Davy on the shoulder and headed back to the idling vehicle which he proceeded to drive into a snow covered field. It wouldn't take him long to clean this up. It wasn't as though this was the first time he had done this sort of thing and he was sure it wouldn't be the last time.

Chapter 31 Bob

The attack on the compound perimeter seemed to peter out then halted completely as a freezing fog began to descend from the mountain tops making the soldiers in the picket line feel even more miserable. Mitch looked up and down the line of mine and rapidly assessed their situation he also noticed the elderly vampire surveying them before vanishing into the swirling fog. They would soon lose their sight lines due to the fog and the ever heavier snow fall. Once that happened the creatures could rush them, it was time to be prudent rather than bold so he gave the obvious order.

"Pull back in buddy units. Once we are at the doorway I want Charlie One reversed back into position. Stubbsy you get her back there and block up the entrance."

A scouse soldier answered in the affirmative over the personal radios. It wasn't long before the engine was gunned and diesel fumes competed with cordite to cloud the area.

The soldiers pulled back swiftly to the compound building joined by the crew from Charlie Two and retreated inside. Finally Charlie One reversed back and Stubbs exited via the rear ramp into the compound building.

"Is everything locked down in Charlie One?" Mitch asked.

"Yes sir. She's as secure as she can be."

"Good lad." He gave Stubbsy a playful clip to the back of his head then looked at the gathered men.

"You know your duties lads. Two men on guard at this entrance at all time on two hour stints. Draw lots or whatever among you but I want everyone to take their turn and to get some rest. McGahan will be along in a minute to take charge. Got that?"

The men responded in various ways but Mitch knew they would work it out and headed to see what had happened with Jamieson.

Mitch reached the room where Jamieson had been held seconds after Bob had arrived holding some gauze to his neck and shoulder. Mitch noted how pissed off Bob looked with himself.

"Did you get caught up in this mess then?"

"No the fucker jumped me while I was on the can." He pointed to the stains on his trousers.

Mitch screwed up his nose. "Did you fall in it?"

Bob nodded, clearly embarrassed. Mitch struggled to hide a smile despite the seriousness of the situation.

"If you two comedians are finished," Joe called over, "we can work out what to do here." He was standing over a scene of carnage. His look of scorn changed to one of concern when he saw the blood on Bob's tunic.

"How badly are you hurt?"

Bob removed the gauze and loosened his tunic so the others could see the extent of his wounds.

"They hurt like hell sir but I think it's just flesh wounds. He never bled on me either so a shot of tetanus should clear it up."

Joe's face paled. "Come on, Bob ... You know that once you are bitten it's a slippery slope."

Bob looked at each of his colleagues in turn, his eyes dark with concern. "I know but it usually takes a couple of days. We just need to last through the night. Once we are back at base I can be quarantined." He paused for effect as he held his gun out to them with the muzzle pointed at his own chest. "Or does one of you want to shoot me right now? I could have kept this hidden from you all you know."

Joe looked towards Mitch but his fellow officer's expression was inscrutable. He knew that Bob could easily have kept this hidden and that boded well for his intentions but they had already paid for not killing someone who was turning. The chances were low that Bob would turn and the only real danger he posed was to himself. The other vampires would zoom in on him if they got into the building. His biggest problem was getting rid of the creature that was once Iain Jamieson. .

"Bob, you are still on duty but the minute you feel anything wrong report it ok? Get yourself down to the civvies. We have set up a med bay next to them."

After he left, Joe spoke to he others "I want to gather a team of four of our smallest troops and bring them to the civvies room. We will need to sit with Steven and get a plan of the air ducts here. We will send this team in after Jamieson. They must kill him in the ducts or flush him out for others to kill. Understood?" He turned away the suddenly stopped.

"Get some of the men to torch Shultz's body in a safe area." Then he headed off to find Steven.

Chapter 32 Whitehall

Forbes picked some imaginary piece of fluff from the sleeve of his crombie coat as he walked the final few yards of the corridor inside the Whitehall office. He would much rather be in the frozen forest near Deil than be in this nest of vipers but when the Home Secretary commanded your presence you had to obey. He nodded curtly at the plain clothes police officer guarding the doorway who opened the door and stepped aside to let him pass. Forbes walked into the office and removed his cloth cap. With the habit of a lifetime he almost stood to attention at the highly polished hardwood desk where the obese home secretary sat. Quentin Quayle had the unfortunate appearance of a decrepit evil toad which was scarily close to his real nature.

Quayle raised an index finger to indicate that Forbes should wait while he finished off typing an email. Forbes stood fuming. This fat idiot had taken him away from the frontline urgently, so urgently he had to leave his men exposed and now he made him wait while he typed. It took a momentous amount of self control to stop himself from bawling out this piece of lard. He doubted that the man had ever had to work for anything in his life. From his low estuary accent through to his sweating neckline sticking over the top of his shirt collar he reeked of privilege and luxury. Forbes despised him and his kind but knew that he needed to kowtow to them.

At long last the short stubby fingers stopped typing and Quayle sat back in his high backed leather chair joining his hands on his expansive belly. As he leant back the shiny patent belt seemed to strain against the pressure from his stomach. He grunted and sniffed as he cleared his throat then began to speak.

"Why is the area not cleared Colonel?"

His piggy little eyes tried to bore into Forbes's but the officer was not easily intimidated especially not by a heart attack in waiting. He focussed for a second on the beads of sweat rolling down Quayle's ruddy cheeks the answered.

"I informed you that it would take perhaps as long as a week to resolve. I have had two days so far." He found it hard to hide his disgust as Quayle picked his nose then leant forward.

"I was told that you were very competent Colonel. Why have you not cleaned up this problem? Do I need to get someone else? Someone more capable? Why is it that I hear instead of cleaning up the problem that your cordon maybe broken?" Forbes managed not to react but he was shocked to realise that the minister knew this, someone in his team must be a spy for the politicians. He would need to discover the mole later but for now he had to concentrate.

"One of our checkpoints believes that one may have escaped. They are not certain though. We have sent helicopter patrols out but they haven't found anything. Nothing could have moved so swiftly as to escape them."

"Do you vouch for that Colonel?"

Forbes could sense a trap closing upon him but he had no choice but to answer.

"Yes I vouch for it."

"Hmm, I wonder." The politician steepled his fingers as he pretended to just think of an idea.

"There is one way of being certain. I want you to give the Broken Arrow order. It is the only way."

Forbes was furious.

"That will be using a sledgehammer to crack a nut. I can clear this up using the tried and tested honeypot tactics."

"No, no, no." Quayle said, he looked up at Forbes with an almost credible impression of sorrow.

"We both know it has gone beyond that. You must give the order Colonel."

He held his hands open.

"Or I will find someone else who will."

Forbes glared at the excuse for a man with unconcealed fury. He let him know that he thought him a loathsome bastard with his eyes, he did not need any words.

"Will that be all Home Secretary?" He snapped.

The politician just waved him away and turned back to his computer screen he needed to check how his bank shares were doing. The unseemly business in Scotland all but forgotten.

Forbes snapped an about turn and stormed out of the room slamming the door behind him and startling the guard at the door. He checked his watch, he had work to do now although he knew from the weather reports that he wouldn't be able to fly back into De'il. He would need to command things from afar. Quayle tutted to himself, the government backed bank shares weren't doing as well as he hoped.

*****

Forbes felt a migraine coming on as he sat in the rear of the chauffeur driven mondeo. He would soon be at the Occult Bureau HQ. Politicians always gave him a headache and the feeling as if he had bathed in shit, he couldn't stand them and their lack of backbone. He fully appreciated that Quayle wanted him to give the order as then there would be no audit trail back to him if some other spineless bastard decided to have an inquest in future years to show the innocence of their parties if and when the x factor generation looked away from their television screens long enough to notice that something happened in the real world. He realised he should call Joe and let him know that the men might have to do a last stand but first of all he would need some insurance just in case and pulled out his mobile phone before ringing a number only he knew.

Chapter 33 Fox Hunt

Steven had a blueprint of the compounds air ducts spread out on a mess table with steel mugs holding down the corners. Joe leant over his shoulder while Mitch and four others including Stubbs looked on. Steven held a pencil in his hand as he gestured to certain points on the system for the benefit of the soldiers. He was thinking furiously as he spoke.

"The only obvious exit to the outside is here. It's pretty near the toilets and is a hatch that hinges up and outwards onto the roof."

"Didn't our men seal that one earlier?" Joe asked.

"Yes but we didn't use holy water like we did on the back door." Damien put in.

"I think this is the way he will try to leave. How clever are they?" Steven asked.

"Some are very clever it depends on how quickly they adapt." Joe said. He was looking at the web of air con tunnels then asked.

"Can this area be sealed off?"

"If he is aiming for that hatch you could climb in just below it where there's a maintenance hatch access."

"Okay, we will get two of the lads in there and Stubbsy I want you and one of the men to enter from the toilets and chase him through."

The four soldiers nodded slowly. They clearly didn't fancy going into tight steel tunnels after a fearsome beast but didn't want to show fear to their commander. Joe looked at Mitch who was clearly unhappy but ordered his men to get to their positions anyway. As the others left Mitch asked.

"Can I have a word Joe?"

"Of course."

"I don't want to question your orders but do you think it's wise risking four more men when we have already lost four out of sixteen?"

"I know but we need to destroy this one before he can cause more damage."

"I hope we don't live to regret this Joe." Mitch patted his superior's arm and they headed after the other soldiers.

****

Stubbs was first to climb up through the maintenance hatch, he scanned around himself using the torch attached to his gun and was relieved to see the tunnels were empty. He hauled himself up and braced himself in the tunnel. He glanced around then noticed the hatch that allowed access to the roof, snow was falling in through its open gap. He looked at this for a moment and edged towards it.

Taking a deep breath to steady himself he looked up through it and saw that the roof was empty. No one was there but it seemed obvious that Jamieson had forced his way out. He ducked back in and closed the hatch behind him then spoke into the comms.

"Stubbs here. Looks like he already left. The hatch was forced open, we will need welding gear here to seal it."

Mitch's voice crackled through to him.

"Roger that Stubbs sit where you are. Second team stand down and get welding gear to Stubbs. Keep in touch with us, the boss and me will be in the mess."

Stubbs jumped at a scraping sound next to him and turned to see his colleague had climbed up behind him. He spoke in his strong cockney accent.

"Alright mate, thought I'd come up and give you some company. Bit parky here innit?"

Stubbs slapped him on the head playfully. Neither of them noticed a set of eyes watching them from further in the darkness of the tunnels before the shape moved silently away. Both soldiers zipped up their smocks further as they waited in the cold.

Chapter 34 Jamieson

Jamieson heard the soothing words of the master in his mind. He understood the instructions and it made sense to the remains of the military man somewhere deep within him. Yes he would follow the two officers and find out their plans so that the master knew how to respond. He crawled along the air ducts being careful to spread his weight and not make a noise. It didn't take long to make his way to the area above the mess and as the master had suspected there was a grille looking down upon the tables. He could see the two officers sitting with Steven.

Mitch spread out the blueprints on the table.

Joe pointed at the diagram. "How secure are the generators and the connection to the main power line Steven? Could the goons possibly get at them?"

All three men hunched over the blueprints now and Steven pointed to an area near toilets.

"The main line connects at the same point as the generators. They are in armoured boxes here that are connected to the main buildings and are surrounded on four sides but the have no roof to allow the fumes to escape into the air. I suppose if they get onto the roofs of the buildings they could get at them but my guess is they don't know where they are because they are hidden among all the service pipes etc in that spot."

Mitch narrowed his eyes. "If they managed to cut them off what would happen to the doors? Would we be trapped inside?"

"No, no. The hydraulic system is just to assist the closing and opening of them. If there is a system failure they can be manually opened but they will be heavy to move. They can still be locked from the inside with the cross bars on them."

"Would the lights just go dark or is there a back up?"

"If for some reason they managed to cut the mains power and the generators then the lights have battery back ups for an emergency situation. We should have twelve to eighteen hours of light."

The men continued to talk but Jamieson had heard enough. He now knew what he needed to do

One of the soldier's spoke over the comms system in a harried tone.

"Major Sir I have Colonel Forbes on the radio for you and he says it's urgent."

Joe got to his feet. "Mitch, get some of the men to check out the power so that we don't get a nasty surprise while I see what news Tim has for us."

"Sure," While Joe raced off to the comms room.

He took the headset from the agitated soldier and listened to his superior. "Joe here sir."

"Joe listen very carefully to me and confirm your understanding," Colonel Forbes said. "You must execute Broken Arrow, I repeat you must execute Broken Arrow. The radar homing device is inside Charlie Two. Drive this to the old church where the university dig was. You must place the device inside so that the bomb can home in on it then try and get as far away as you can. I am sorry to leave you in this shitty situation but the spineless twats in Whitehall want to brush this under the carpet immediately. Do you understand your orders?"

Joe was taken aback, he always knew that he might face this situation some day but secretly had hoped he never would. He realised that Tim was waiting his proper response.

"I uh, I hear you clearly Tim and understand."

"God speed Joe I pray that you all make it out of range of the blast."

The connection was broken abruptly at the other end. Joe took several deep breaths in an effort to control his racing heart. He now had to follow the orders that he had been given and he had to do this immediately. He took off the headset and carefully placed it on the radio set while he collected his thoughts. He clicked on his throat mike and spoke to all of the people inside the building.

"Attention I want all soldiers to prepare to meet in the mess immediately. That is a direct order."

Chapter 35 A Bomber Launches

The lights on the long runway in Cambridgeshire were barely visibly through the darkness and the heavy rain as Josh Hunt taxied the heavily laden Tornado bomber onto it and prepared to fire up the afterburners to full power. He and his navigator listened intently as they received clearance to take off from the control tower. Within seconds the powerful jet was rocketing along the concrete runway and soared into the heavily laden sky headed for Scotland. With any luck they would be back in time to enjoy a hearty breakfast.

Chapter 36 Broken Arrow Explained

There was an expectant murmur from the people gathered in the mess as the waited on their commander speaking. Joe surveyed the small crowd then said to Mitch.

"Who's missing?"

"Stubbs and Reid are checking the power. Everyone else is here." Joe nodded at this shuffled his feet and spoke in a clear voice.

"Ladies and Gentlemen, just as we thought things couldn't get any worse the politicians have begun to meddle. They want us to clear up this mess pronto. We have to initiate operation Broken Arrow. All of the soldiers here know what this means but for the rest of us it means that an order has been given to bomb our positions. Usually done when we are being overrun. In this case vampires might be breaching the cordon."

Claire looked at Tom who remained impassive.

"We will split into two groups. Essentially you will go with the squad in Charlie one along with the civilians to the church at Cothqon to wait on Charlie two which will contain the rest of the troops under my command. Mitch you know what my orders will be. I have to plant the Broken Arrow device at the old church where the uni dig was then high tail it to meet up with you. All going well we will all leave at high speed through the base camp to the real world. If for any reason things aren't going to plan I want you to leave directly to keep the civilians safe. There is no time for questions so get Stubbs and Reid back here and everything squared up for leaving in five minutes. Chop chop." He clapped his hands together in emphasis of the final point.

The assembled people did not need to be told twice they headed off to pick up their essential equipment. Tom and Claire exchanged glances as they ran to pick up their parkas from the room.

****

Stubbs was on the roof of the compound having climbed out of the grille when Mitch's voice came through their personal comms ordering them back. He ducked his head back in the air conditioning tunnel to ask Reid if he had heard their orders but the other soldier was nowhere to be seen. He dropped back in and closed the grille behind him before using his torch to illuminate the tunnels. The light reflected from some small splashes of blood and he immediately realised what had happened to Reid and that he was in serious trouble.

He double tapped his throat mike and spoke rapidly. "Joe this is Stubbs. I think Jamieson is still in the air con tunnels. Reid is missing. I'm on my way back." He had turned a corner and came face to face with Jamieson. Oh shit …"

The creature was too close for him to bring his weapon up to bear and the mouth opened to an impossible angle hissing foul breath into the soldier's face. Stubbs had to go for it though. He swung the gun as quickly as he could but the vampire managed to clamp its jaws round his throat and bit down viciously. Stubbs howled in agony as he pulled on the trigger of his gun and at least felt the satisfaction of the bullets hitting into the vampire's torso. Jamieson bit into his own lips spitting some of his blood into Stubbs' mouth he then staggered backwards staring down at his disintegrating body as it swiftly changed to ash and blew apart. Stubbs ripped off his body armour and left out a little anguished sob, he had come so far and now it was going to finish in a dark corner in the middle of nowhere. He pulled out the cross that hung round his neck and kissed it before letting it drop. He muttered.

"Hope this works."

In one swift sure movement he raised his gun and fired it into his chest. His dead limp body collapsed to the floor of the air con tunnels and he could no longer hear the desperate calling of Joe's voice from his personal comms.

****

Joe slapped the wall of the portakabin in frustration as he heard the report of Stubbs's gun. He knew that neither Stubbs or Reid would be joining him on the mission to the dig site.

"Shit, shit, shit." He shouted in frustration and kicked the wall before composing himself. Too many good people had died in these hills. He clicked on his comms and shouted for the rest of his men.

"Come on guys hurry it up we must be in Charlie two in one minute."

Joe already had all the kit he needed attached to him and the broken arrow equipment was in Charlie two so he didn't mess around he just unslung his gun and headed to the vehicle where he was happy to see Bob Jones in the drivers seat gunning the engine. The three other soldiers Del Carey, Brian Roderick and Corporal Paul Slavin all followed swiftly after. The ramp hissed upwards as Paul entered.

"Charlie one is already off Sir." Bob declared over the comms. Joe just patted him on the shoulder as he surged the APC towards the exit from the compound. Joe looked at the anxious faces of his section. They were good solid men but they all knew that this was almost a suicide mission. To get close enough with the broken arrow device they would need to go into the heart of the vampire's nest. The chances of surviving that weren't worth writing home about. He could tell that each of them was making their peace with the world before they faced their doom and he was in no mood to disturb them but he needed to.

"Carey and Roderick you cover me and Bob while we go into the church. Slavin I want you to take over the wheel and get ready to hightail it as soon as we come running out."

They all knew there was no chance Joe and Bob would be coming out but they all nodded accepting the lie for the bravado that it was and proceeded to check their personal kit once more. Joe walked to the back of the vehicle and checked inside the armoured box that the broken arrow transmitter was ready for deployment. The bomber would be orbiting somewhere above anytime soon so he needed to be certain. The drill was to switch it on and check the transmitter beeped twice followed by a low hum confirming the aircraft had locked on then he had to switch it to standby before turning the switch once more back to active when it was on site. Joe followed the drill and was satisfied everything was in order, it would need to be.

Chapter 37 Back to Cothqon

Inside Charlie one, McGahan fired the .50 cal gun in the turret as the APC raced along the forest road back to Cothqon. He shot anything that moved to ensure they had a clear path while the driver raced the vehicle along at breakneck speed almost losing the tracks a few times he was going so fast.

Mitch looked around the vehicle and saw the grim expressions of his soldiers. He knew they would fight till overrun but the civvies were another thing. The two police officers seemed okay to him although he thought Claire looked openly scared but that was no bad thing. Steven looked terrified while Damien and Teresa took turns talking into one another's ears and nodding a lot. He felt a bit frightened of the confidence those two had. They reminded him so much of the boss, that same certainty that they would prevail. If only he could have some of that self belief. He realised that Teresa was looking at him with concern, her soft features spread into a warm smile which Mitch couldn't help but return and suddenly he felt better.

The vehicle slewed to a halt outside the chapel house and McGahan did a quick scan with the sensors.

"It seems clear ...."

Mitch took a second, now was the crucial moment. He had to decide on whether they stay in the vehicle or hold up in the church to wait on Charlie two. He was weighing it up when Teresa's voice came over the comms.

"They want to trap us in the church!"

Damien tapped her shoulder and then spoke through the comms as well.

"I would like to pick up my historical records that are in the chapel house, they cover the vampire activity over several years. I don't think we should leave it to be destroyed."

Mitch wasn't keen on risking everyone for paperwork but he knew the Boss wouldn't want to lose the records.

"Okay we go in quick as a team and come back out quick. No messing about. Understood?"

Everyone nodded. They all prepared themselves as the ramp hissed down. Two of the soldiers ran forward to cover the entrance to the chapel house and waited while Damien poured some holy water on the door handles. The water gave off a dull glow for a second then settled. Damien's brow furrowed deeply. Noticing this Tom asked.

"Are we safe?"

Damien looked beyond him to Mitch.

"I don't know but I think so."

Mitch gave a gesture to his men and they opened the doors and entered the house.

"Where's the records Father?"

"In the front sitting room." Damien answered and led the way with a close bodyguard. They walked along the hall and into the sitting room without incident. Seeing the room was empty Damien let out a short gasp and walked over to his overturned desk. He opened a drawer and removed several DVDs and raised them above his head.

"I had the records put on DVD recently. We move with the times."

Claire couldn't help smiling at the elderly priest being up to date with technology.

"Is that everything?" Mitch asked.

"One more thing." Damian said. He knelt next to the desk disconnecting something and appeared with an external hard drive. "Back up." He explained.

"Ok let's go guys. I think we are pushing our luck now."

Everyone agreed and turned to leave as swiftly as they could. They were just leaving the house when Steven noticed movement to their right. A vampire had escaped their notice earlier, he was racing along the ceiling towards Teresa at a great rate. As the creature jumped from the ceiling Steven rugby tackled him in a desperate effort to save the girl. He felt rushes of air as the vampire snapped at him and gagged at his rancid breath while they rolled about the floor. Steven elbowed his opponent hard in the side of his head but still the vampire fought furiously. The soldiers tried to aim their guns but the two fighters were moving so swiftly it was impossible to get a clear shot for fear of shooting Steven.

On one of their rolls Steven noticed that the sun had begun to rise outside and decided to use this. He used his shoulders to roll further out the door. The vampire realised too late what was happening and could not save himself but in a final malevolent act head butted Steven then tore a chunk out of his neck with his canines. The sunlight seared into the vampire boiling his insides and roasting his skin. This blackened and curled upwards like old parchment, his mouth opened in a silent scream his head bent backwards while his body exploded in flames then dissolved in front of their eyes.

Claire and Mitch ran forward to check on Steven who sat on the door step holding his torn neck. His head was bowed in despair. Teresa leant forward and placed a tiny hand on his cheek. Steven smiled sadly at her, admiring how deep the child's eyes were.

"He bit me, I'm going to turn aren't I?"

Teresa nodded and Mitch spoke for them all.

"You saved us Steven but you are marked now."

"What do we do?" Claire asked, she looked round the others.

"You need to leave me." Steven said with finality. "When the bomb's dropped I won't know anything. I don't want to become one of those things."

Teresa stroked his cheek then kissed it while the others took it in turns to pat him on the shoulder. No-one knew what to say. Claire took one last look at their desperately sad colleague while the APC ramp closed behind her.

"Take us down through the camp and head out of the hills." Ordered Mitch as the APC raced off while Steven rocked back and forwards on his knees sobbing to himself.

Chapter 38 Charlie Two and the End Game

Charlie Two drew up outside the entrance to the old church where the trouble had all begun. Joe took a deep breath. They had managed so far without incident but he knew the vampires wouldn't let them get any further without a fight and he and Bob were more than likely going to meet their deaths in the next few minutes. They both removed their flak vests ostensibly to allow them to move faster while carrying the broken arrow device but no one in the vehicle was fooled by that. They all knew that it would allow them to be certain they could shoot each other if they had to. He wanted to savour his last moments of peace and pulled out his cross before kissing it then replacing it with a silent prayer for strength and courage. He locked eyes with Bob who nodded then moved from the driver's seat to let Slavin in.

The two old comrades each grabbed a handle on opposite sides of the broken arrow device and braced themselves as the ramp hissed down. Carey and Roderick stood either side of them guns up at the aim and stepped out first to provide covering fire.

It was deathly quiet as they scanned the small slopes around them and walked down the steps inside the church entrance.

"Ok guys guard the top of the stairs and we'll go in." Joe tried to sound calm but felt his voice was several octaves higher with tension. In his peripheral vision he could see the two men take up covering positions. There was no hesitating now, he and Bob had to get into the uncovered chamber and let the bomber do its job. He turned the switch on the device to activate once more and they jogged down the steep stairwell. Their path then took a sharp turn to the left and they were amazed to see the generators were still working to give light for them which was a god send. They reached a cold damp corridor and saw the dark break in the wall at the far end where they needed to go. They switched on torches attached to their smocks and walked on.

The creature that had once been the professor sat in the darkness of the chamber waiting on the soldiers with a small number of his brethren. The master had told him this was a most important task and that they must not halt the soldiers' progress. He didn't truly understand why they should let the soldiers in but he must obey his master.

It didn't take long for Joe and Bob to haul the device down to a circular chamber which was dissected by a shallow depression rather like a canal. They placed the device beside this and looked around with their torches in their hands.

"Do you think this is where they were imprisoned Joe?" Bob kept his voice hushed afraid it would carry too far. Joe nodded his reply as he walked towards the depression. He flashed his torch around and saw a large iron cross against the wall.

"Yeah this is where it began and where it ends." He said almost to himself before adding. "I think we should get back to the APC."

The words had no sooner left his lips when Bob shouted a warning. Joe ducked a second too late to avoid the hurtling dark figure catching him. What was once a woman screamed as she smacked him a very hard punch knocking him off his feet. He rolled hard to his left desperately unslinging his gun before he recovered into a kneeling position and aimed at her. She erupted into flames in front of his eyes as Bob beat him to the draw. He swivelled his gun to the left and let rip at a further group of advancing vampires.

Several miles above the fire fight Josh Hunt kept the bomber in a lazy wide turn as his weapons officer concentrated intently on his screen in the rear seat. After a couple of seconds he heard the words he had been waiting for over the intercom. "Bombs gone!"

****

The bomber lifted several feet as the heavy bomb hurtled towards the ground. Josh fleetingly thought of the soldiers below and hoped they got out of the blast zone in time then his thoughts turned to the breakfast that would be waiting for him back at the base as he swept the aircraft's wings back fully and engaged the afterburner. The bomber accelerated away into the brightening sky.

****

Carey and Roderick looked at one another when they heard the gunfire. Carey charged down the steps followed swiftly by Roderick. They wouldn't leave their comrades alone.

Bob couldn't believe it. In all his long military career he had never known a Heckler and Koch weapon to jam but here he was surrounded by enemies and his HK53 had suffered a stoppage. Keeping calm he dropped the weapon and reached for his pistol, too late. One of the creatures grabbed the rim of his helmet and used it to snap his head back while a second bit deep into his neck. He screamed in pain then shouted to Joe.

"Shoot, for Christ sake shoot me!"

Joe howled in despair as he emptied the remainder of his magazine into the surging mass of bodies. The vampires dissolved and Bob slumped to the cold damp floor lifeless. Joe hadn't time to mourn his friend as he needed to reload before the next group of vampires attacked.

He slammed home the magazine but didn't need it. Carey and Roderick let rip firing into the last charge by the vampires. The creatures disappeared in a greasy cloud which rapidly dissipated. Joe ran towards his men and they all raced for the surface.

Slavin gunned the engine loudly and lowered the ramp to allow the three men to enter at a fast canter. As soon as they were in Joe shouted above the noise for them to leave. Slavin had them racing away before the ramp had even closed. Joe gave a thumbs up to Carey and Roderick and pulled on the radio headset to talk to Joe.

"Charlie two on their way Mitch. We are one man down, Bob was killed down in the church."

There was a long moment of static then Mitch answered.

"Okay Sir get your arses out of there we are already on our way out of the hills. I'll get you a nice cold beer back at the base. Over and out."

The connection abruptly died so Joe turned off the set and sat in one of the seats as the APC bounced along the forest roads towards Cothqon.

Slavin was screwing his eyes against the snow to try and peer through it to see the way ahead. For a split second he thought the sun had suddenly risen in the wrong place.

The bomb surged through the earth for several feet at fantastic speed, Its armoured nose doing its job and preventing instant detonation. After it reached deep enough to destroy most enemy bunkers the nuclear chain reaction began that swiftly lead to the inevitable explosion the weapon was designed for. The resulting blast and shockwave picked up the APC and hurled it into the forest as if it were a child's toy scattering many of the trees that were being uprooted by the blast. The men inside bounced about trying desperately to protect themselves to no avail. By the time the vehicle came to rest against a particularly dense clump of fallen trees only

Joe had survived and he knew by the pain he felt all over his body that he wasn't in a good way. He didn't have long to think this over before the heat blast hit the vehicle turning it instantly into a powerful oven and roasting the unfortunate officer alive. The only fortunate thing for him was that it was quick. An instant of searing heat and light then nothing as the blast carried on out in its ever widening radius.

In the forest around Charlie Two several vampires were incinerated in their lairs while they slumbered. They had the undeserved luxury of being blissfully unaware as the flames devoured them. The blast and firestorm from the nuclear bomb seemed to be finding them no matter where they had sought refuge. Steven gave out a little sigh as the sky brightened intensely around him realising he wasn't going to feel the horror of turning into one of those creatures then he felt a great sense of nothingness.

Chapter 39 Debriefing

Claire sat on a hard backed plastic chair staring at her feet. The interview room she was in couldn't be much more than 9 metres square and had a small plastic table between her and a seat that was a twin of her own. It was lit by a single fluorescent light that reflected dully off the battleship grey walls. *Jesus this must be what suspects feel like in the station.* She mused. There was nothing of interest in the room to break up the monotony of waiting.

Footsteps in the corridor outside disturbed her melancholy and the steel backed door opened in towards her. She almost leapt for joy when she saw Tom and Mitch enter the room especially as they were unaccompanied. She held out her arms horizontally.

"Well?"

Tom looked at Mitch who explained.

"You are both free to return home. The Military Police seem satisfied that you will adhere to the Official Secrets Act and that you are trustworthy citizens. I imagine we will all be under surveillance for a while but I don't think any of us will want to discuss this anyway."

"Plus who is going to believe any of us if we decide to blab?" Tom added.

"Best case is that some of the people who follow the conspiracy theories would mention us in their websites. I think it is best we all forget what happened and get on with our lives as best we can."

Mitch's face betrayed no emotion as he looked from one Police officer to the other. He coughed and straightened his uniform.

"We aren't sure if our unit will be disbanded. I have been told that the Boss is going to carry the can for this so they will either scatter our unit to the four winds or keep us together to watch us closely. The army's my home though so I think I will just need to keep my head down and get on with it. I am being allowed to keep my commission so I am an officer again but God knows where I will be sent but I'm one of the lucky ones. I can't believe the Boss is getting the blame of all this."

He slowly shook his head then looked at them both in turn.

"I just wanted to say goodbye and thanks to you both. I can't imagine we'll see one another again."

Claire sat forward.

"What's happening to Damian and Teresa?"

"Teresa will go to an orphanage with Damian becoming one of her tutors. Unfortunately I think the army is going to take special interest in her as she grows up because of her powers. Poor little thing."

He made an exaggerated gesture of looking at his watch.

"I'm sorry but I must be going and my superiors won't like it if I'm late. Good bye and good luck."

Claire surged forward and hugged Mitch tightly. He patted her on the back and then they separated. He looked very bashful and waved to them both as he left the room. Claire turned to Tom.

"So what happens now?"

He nodded towards the open door.

"We go out the front door to get a car waiting on us that will take us back to the station. One good thing is we won't be debriefed there because it is all being brushed under the carpet. I think the Inspector will want to chat to us for a bit then we can head home to our beds."

"Don't think I'll sleep much." Claire said leaving the room.

"Me neither." Tom agreed as he closed the door behind them.

****

Colonel Tim Forbes sipped on a glass of iced water as he sat in the main television room of the Guards Club staring at the large plasma screen in silence. He felt more alone and despairing than he ever had before in his life even though there were several other senior officers sitting in the widely spaced high wing backed chairs and couches in the dimly lit room. The BBC News channel was playing a loop of amateur film showing a distant mushroom cloud with a reporter's voice over informing the public that an RAF bomber carrying a nuclear bomb had crashed in the Scottish Borders. Forbes shook his head sadly for he knew that most of the brain dead population would accept that story as they ate their breakfast while waiting on the latest results of the votes on some reality show or other. The politicians had their backs covered while good men and women had died. He also had the nagging thought that at least one vampire had escaped the cordon area. Oh how ironic it would be if the only concrete result of the quarantine operation was to help an ancient evil escape into the wider world. He looked up as someone coughed to his side.

Two armed military policemen stood in their smartly pressed uniforms and highly polished boots. He could actually smell the bees wax polish from them as he stood smartly. These men had certainly never seen combat before but at least the lieutenant seemed to be unhappy about what they were doing as he spoke softly but firmly.

"Sir, would you mind coming with us? I assume we don't need to handcuff you."

"No you don't son. I'll come peacefully." He buttoned up his tunic and put on his officer's cap as he left his office flanked by the two parade soldiers. Thankfully he had the foresight to call in his insurance before the policeman had arrived.

Epilogue

Quentin Quayle wolfed down a croissant slathered in full fat butter leaving half the greasy spread on his jowls. He grunted to himself as he read the morning mail given to him by his secretary. He guffawed as he read the report on Colonel Tim Forbes being court martialled and sent to a military prison for misconduct during an exercise in the Scottish Borders. That would teach the upstart. He instinctively despised working class men who got above their station. His family had spent generations in powerful positions and knew how to rule. These working class peasants should know their place. He sniggered once more then his jaw fell open with butter grease dripping down as he looked at the contents of a brown envelope addressed for his personal attention.

Several high quality black and white photographs slid across his desk. They showed the younger but unmistakeable figure of the Right Honourable Quentin Quayle Home Secretary with a boy who was clearly underage along with several shots of him in various compromising positions in a public toilet with different young boys. Trying to control the shake of his hands and the hammering of his overworked heart he sifted through the photographs to pick up some notepaper with Army letterhead. He turned it over with his short stubby fingers and read the spider like handwriting which read:

Thought you might find these images "interesting" old chap. I have several people throughout the civilised world ready to deliver these to the scandal rags if I am not at liberty within six months or if a strange accident should happen to me.

Look forward to seeing you once you organise my release. Better get on the phone QQ.

Tim

Quayle choked as he tried to swallow a piece of croissant too quickly. That bastard had set him up. After a few seconds of struggling he managed to dislodge it then stared at the photographs and note. He sat sweating profusely for a moment, then ever the pragmatist he made up his mind on how to protect his career. He put the items back in the envelope then pressed his intercom. His secretary answered immediately and Quayle bellowed.

"Get me the Army Chief of Staff."

This wasn't going to be a good day for Quentin Quayle but he would never forgive or forget this meddling army officer.

Printed in Great Britain
by Amazon